OVER THE FENCE

ADVENTURES IN FRIENDSHIP

Over the Fence
Published by Orange, a division of The reThink Group, Inc.
5870 Charlotte Lane, Suite 300
Cumming, GA 30040 U.S.A.
The Orange logo is a registered trademark of The reThink Group, Inc.

Other Orange products are available online and direct from the publisher. Visit our
website at www.ThinkOrange.com for more resources like these.

ISBN: 978-1-941259-14-6

©2014 The reThink Group, Inc.

Writers: Elizabeth Hansen, Dan Scott, Lauren Terrell
Editorial Team: Mike Clear, Kristen Ivy, Jennifer Wilder, Tim Walker
Art Direction: Ryan Boon
Design: Joe Goode (cover), Brian Bascle (interior art), Hudson Phillips (layout)

Printed in the United States of America
First Edition 2014

2 3 4 5 6 7 8 9 10 11

09/02/2015

TABLE OF CONTENTS

HEY THERE!

You may be wondering what you've just picked up. Is it a story? A devotional? Something your dog will chew up if you leave it on the floor?

Yes, yes and maybe yes. Depends on whether you smear bacon grease on the pages.

BOTTOM LINE: this is a book about friendship. And it's based on what the Bible has to say about being a true friend. Someone once asked Jesus to name the very most important thing to do when you follow God. Jesus actually listed two important things to do:

LOVE GOD.
LOVE OTHERS.

So, being a good friend is the second most important thing you can do, right? Well, yes. But get this: One of the ways you can show your love for God is by loving others, too. So friendship is also part of the *most* important thing you'll ever do.

Sometimes friendship seems to come easily, almost by accident. But sometimes your friends can drive you crazy, too! God knows that, so He has laid out a plan for friendship that includes a lot of "each others"—things like "love each other," "encourage each other," and "serve each other." Each week for the next nine weeks, you'll explore a new "each other."

So, where do I start?

Glad you asked! Each week features an episode about four friends on a mission to discover what's behind a mysterious fence in the woods. The toughest part of their adventure isn't climbing the fence—it's figuring out how to make their friendship work.

Start off the week with Day One—reading the episode. Then, over the next four days, dive into the devotional activities and questions based on what our four friends learned in that week's episode. You might find yourself running around barefoot in the mud. Or planning a sleepover. Or even making breakfast.

ENJOY THE ADVENTURE.
AND INVITE YOUR FRIENDS TO JOIN YOU!

A NEW YORK CHANGE OF PLANS

Even before hopping out of bed, Emma checked the weather app on her phone. A bright yellow sun winked, letting her know it would be a clear day with temperatures in the 80s. "Perfect!" she exclaimed, bouncing to her feet.

Emma's mom grinned from the doorway. "You could just look out the window, you know."

Emma shook out her tangled hair as she changed into her favorite T-shirt with a kitten on it. She bounded for the door. "Can I pack a lunch for me and Ethan? To take with us in the woods?"

Emma's mom shook her head. "There's been . . . a change of plans."

"But you said we could explore!" Emma protested. She and her best friend, Ethan, had planned out the entire summer, down to the very last detail. How could her mom turn things upside down on the very first day of vacation?

Sitting down on the edge of the bed, Emma's mom sighed. "We're having a guest. Your cousin, Lily."

Emma frowned. "Lily? From New York City?" It had been years since Emma had seen her cousin, back when they were just little kids. Emma mostly remembered tall buildings and loud traffic from their visit to New York. Lily had seemed to know exactly what was going on all the time, while Emma felt lost, even with her family right there.

"Yes," Emma's mom nodded. "Dad's picking her up at the train station now."

"Are Aunt Jill and Uncle Ted coming, too?" Emma's mind raced as she considered all the things she and Ethan had planned for the summer. "Lily won't be here long, right?"

Emma's mom hesitated for a moment, and then put her hand on Emma's shoulder. "Well . . . probably the whole summer."

Emma could only stare, speechless. She wanted to protest, but it sounded as though Lily was already on the way. The grown-ups had sorted it all out without asking Emma what she thought. And now she was the one who would have to live with it.

Later, Emma and Ethan held an emergency meeting on his back porch. "We were supposed to have the whole summer to explore the woods!" Emma grumbled.

"Yeah!" Ethan agreed. "And find out what's behind . . . The Fence."

They both paused, listening to the faint construction sounds that filtered through the forest. Just last week, they had discovered a brand-new, high wooden fence on the other side of the woods. Something mysterious was being built, and they were determined to discover what it was. Ethan frowned as he fiddled with his rock climbing gear.

"Maybe your cousin could just come along with us," he suggested.

"Ha!" Emma scoffed. She couldn't imagine Lily plunging through the brush. Her cousin would probably worry too much about breaking a perfectly polished fingernail. "Wait 'til you meet her."

The honk of a car horn next door cut off the rest of her thoughts. "There they are," Emma groaned. "I gotta go."

Reluctantly, Emma returned to her own yard as her dad's car pulled into the driveway. She took a deep breath as Lily stepped out. "Uh oh," she murmured under her breath. Her cousin was just as bad as Emma had imagined. Worse.

Lily was wearing a sequined tank top, bejeweled jeans, and high-heeled sandals. Her hair was smooth and glossy with a streak of deep purple down the side. She looked way older, even though Emma knew they were both 11.

Emma's mom breezed past her to offer Lily a warm hug. "Lily!" she exclaimed. "We're so glad to have you."

Lily didn't seem any more excited to be here than Emma was to have her. "Hi, Aunt Liz," she murmured.

As dad dragged Lily's enormous suitcase toward the house, Lily and Emma were left facing each other. Lily stared at Emma's kitten T-shirt. "I had a shirt like that," she commented. "In kindergarten."

Emma felt her face redden as she glanced down at her ratty T-shirt. It suddenly seemed over-cute. Just like something a little kid would wear. "I like it," she said defensively.

Lily glanced down the street. "You have a lot of grass. And trees."

"Yeah." Emma let her words hang. It was an ordinary neighborhood with lawns and woods and a corner field for soccer. What did Lily expect?

"It's so, like . . . quiet out here. What do you do?"

Emma took a deep breath. She ought to be nice and tell Lily all about the adventures she and Ethan had planned. But what came out of her mouth instead was, "Probably nothing you'd care about."

"Emma!" her mom warned. "Show Lily your room. She's sharing with you."

Emma bit her tongue to keep from groaning. It was official: Summer was ruined, before it even started. She sighed as she ushered Lily to the front porch, up the stairs, and into her room.

Though Emma had always loved her room, she couldn't help seeing it now through her cousin's eyes. The little alcove with the window seat was perfect for reading, but the curtains still had the hearts and rainbows Emma had picked out when she was four. One wall was covered with a huge whiteboard where Emma scribbled pictures and diagrams of the machines she took apart, like toasters and old flip phones. Lily's walls were probably plastered with boy band posters.

Sure enough, Lily frowned as she noted the nest of electrical equipment on Emma's desk. "What's with all the gadgets and wires and things?" she asked.

Emma wanted to explain how much fun it was to take something apart and figure out how it worked. How building a robot was way more satisfying to her than putting on a layer of nail polish. Instead, Emma simply shrugged. "I like to fix things. And research stuff. C'mon, let me show you the house."

Lily stared in surprise as Emma ushered her into the den. "That's your TV? It's so small. Ours takes up a whole wall." Emma's lips tightened into a thin line.

At lunch, Emma's mom served her famous lasagna. "How much would you like, Lily?" she asked.

Lily shook her head. "I don't eat meat."

It was Emma's turn to stare. "No hamburgers? No bacon?" Emma couldn't imagine Saturday mornings without her Dad's bacon and waffles or Fourth of July without her Uncle Jesse's famous barbecued ribs.

Lily crossed her arms. "You shouldn't eat that stuff either. It's, like, really bad for your heart."

Emma simmered. What if her mom and dad decided that being nice to Lily meant no meat for their family, either? She had to talk to someone, right away. Sliding her phone from her pocket, she quickly texted Ethan under the table:

"MEET. OAK. 15 MIN."

Though Emma's mom was at the counter making peanut butter and jelly for Lily, she somehow still knew when Emma was texting. "No screens at the table!" she said firmly. "And I want you to help Lily unpack as soon as we're done eating."

After lunch, Emma waited until Lily was in the bathroom. Then she snuck out the patio doors and slid along the side of the house. She was so intent on getting to the big oak on the edge of the woods that she didn't notice her mom weeding in the flowerbed.

"Young lady, I told you to help Lily!" her mom called, digging out a stubborn dandelion.

Emma stood her ground as she watched all hope of escape disappear. "Yeah, well, Lily doesn't need me. She doesn't like anything here!"

"That's no reason to sneak out and leave her behind," Emma's mom pointed out.

"She's ruined the whole summer!" Emma declared. It felt good to say it out loud after thinking it so many times all day.

Her mom's voice softened. "Emma, things are hard for Lily at home right now. Aunt Jill and Uncle Ted are . . . they're not getting along very well."

Emma sighed. She was so frustrated with her cousin that she didn't want to try seeing things from Lily's point of view. But Emma had a good imagination, and it started wondering before she could stop it. What would it be like if things weren't happy at home? What would it be like if she suddenly had to pack up and go to New York City for a whole summer? Well, it still didn't make it fair for Emma.

Finally Emma asked, "So . . . you're gonna make me take Lily along?"

Emma's mom simply nabbed Emma's phone from her pocket and dropped it in her hand. "Mom," Emma protested. "Don't get dirt on it!"

Shaking her head, Mom laughed. "I'm thinking with all these fancy apps, you've got at least one that can help you be a good cousin. And friend." Dusting off her hands, mom reached over and tapped Emma's Bible app. "Try First John. Right here."

Emma focused on the screen and slowly read the words aloud. "'What is love? It is not that we loved God. It is that he loved us and sent his Son to give his life to pay for our sins. Dear friends, since

God loved us that much, we should also love one another. If we love one another, God lives in us. His love is made complete in us.'"

Emma took a deep breath. "I sure don't feel like loving Lily," she said.

"That's okay," her mom replied. "You can still treat her in a loving way. In fact, sometimes when you act in a loving way, you start feeling it, too."

Slowly, Emma nodded. Back inside, she found her cousin curled up on the second twin bed. Lily tried to smile brightly, but it was clear she'd been crying.

"All these weird trees," Lily sniffed. "They're, like, making my eyes water."

Emma handed her a tissue. "Me and my friend Ethan are going exploring back in all those weird trees. You wanna come with us?" she asked.

For a moment, Lily perked up. Then she glanced down at her

sparkly outfit. "I, um . . . not really."

"That's all right." Emma grinned. "I've got some old sneakers. Oh, and a T-shirt. If you don't mind one with a puppy on it."

Lily cracked a tiny smile. "I've always wanted a puppy! We just can't get one 'cause we live five floors up."

"Well, c'mon!" Emma jumped up. "Ethan's got a beagle puppy."

After Lily changed, the two girls hurried outside and across the backyard toward the big oak. Emma still wasn't sure what she thought about her cousin. But maybe the summer wouldn't be a total disaster, after all. ■

DAY 2

Love. For such a mushy-gushy word, we sure do use it a lot. Don't believe it? Take a second to fill in the blanks of the following statements with one of these phrases:

LOVE
DON'T CARE ABOUT
CAN'T STAND

I .... **BACON.**

I .... **ONE DIRECTION.**

I .... **3D MOVIES.**

I .... **ROLLERCOASTERS.**

I .... **CANDY.**

It's probably safe to say, you wrote "LOVE" in at least one of those blanks and even safer to say you've uttered a similar statement declaring your love in the last 24 hours. The word *love* is part of our everyday language, but what does it really mean? To help answer that question, write the names of three people who love you.

1.
....

2.
....

3.
....

Now, take a minute to think about how you know that person loves you. Is it something they say? Is it something they do? Is it the time they spend with you or gifts they have given you?

The cool thing about love is that we know how to love others because we are loved. And what's even cooler is that we *all* have the exact same example of the most perfect love. Check out this verse from 1 John 4:10-12:

> *What is love? It is not that we loved God. It is that he loved us and sent his Son to give his life to pay for our sins. Dear friends, since God loved us that much, we should also love one another. No one has ever seen God. But if we love one another, God lives in us. His love is made complete in us.*

How cool is that? God has shown us His love so that we know how to love others. That means every time you show someone love, every time someone shows they love you, it's because God first loved us and showed us what real love is!

It's important to show love to everyone from your mom to your Starbucks barista, but this month is all about friendship. And love is a major ingredient in friendship. Because **friends love each other.**

❂ SO, WHAT DOES THIS MEAN TO YOU? TAKE A FEW MINUTES AND THINK ABOUT THE WAY GOD LOVES YOU AND THE WAY HE SHOWS HIS LOVE FOR YOU THROUGH THE PEOPLE AROUND YOU. WRITE DOWN A FEW WAYS YOU COULD SHOW YOUR FRIENDS THAT SAME LOVE.

....

....

....

....

....

DAY 3

If you're like most kids, you have to follow a bunch of rules. Maybe you've been told to always write your name on the upper right-hand corner of your homework. Maybe you need to make your bed every day or eat at least one helping of veggies at dinner.

What are some of the rules you have to follow? Write a few of them here:

....

....

....

Why do you think you have those rules? Is it because grown-ups are bored and love to see what they can get you to do? Or could it be that those rules are meant to keep you safe and learn how to get along with people around you?

You might not feel this way right now, but rules are pretty important. Back when Jesus was on the earth, God's people, the Jews, had a ton of rules—613, to be exact.

Yeah, insane.

So one day, a teacher of all of those 613 rules asked Jesus which of them was the most important. Jesus broke it down for the people listening. Check out Jesus' answer in Matthew 22:37-39:

> *"Love the Lord your God with all your heart and with all your soul. Love him with all your mind." This is the first and most important commandment. And the second is like it. "Love your neighbor as you love yourself."*

Jesus took those 613 rules and summarized them with just a few simple ideas:

LOVE GOD.
LOVE YOURSELF THE WAY GOD LOVES YOU.
LOVE OTHERS THE WAY GOD LOVES THEM.

That's a lot simpler than 613 rules, huh? So, it all comes down to love. And really, it all comes down to loving God. Because when you really love God, you are going to love all the things He has made—like you and the people around you! Think about it: **Isn't loving our friends a way we can love God?**

God made your friends and the people in your life and He loves them very much. So, instead of trying to keep track of all the rules in your life, try to focus on loving God and all the people He has made. (And yes, loving your mom might mean making your bed like she wants.) And remember, loving your friends is a way you can love God.

◑ TAKE A MINUTE AND WRITE DOWN A FUN WAY YOU CAN DO THESE THREE THINGS:

LOVE GOD

....

LOVE YOURSELF

....

LOVE OTHERS

....

NOW, MAKE A PLAN AND GET TO IT. SHOW THE KIND OF LOVE THAT PEOPLE WILL NEVER FORGET!

DAY 4

It's time to listen to some music. Grab your music and head to the nearest speaker system in your house. Pick your favorite song and get it ready to play. But don't press PLAY yet! First, crank the volume to the loudest it can go. (You may want to ask your parents first or warn anyone standing nearby.) Now . . . if you dare, press PLAY.

I bet it wasn't too long before you had to turn off the music—or a parent came running into the room to find out what in the world you were doing.

The music was pretty loud, wasn't it? Probably loud enough that you couldn't talk to anyone without shouting. Loud enough that someone couldn't get your attention. Maybe even so loud that you didn't enjoy listening to your favorite song.

Just because it's loud, doesn't mean it's good.

Did you know that the same goes for the good things we try to do for others?

Check out this part of a letter that Paul, one of Jesus' first followers, wrote to a church in the ancient city of Corinth:

> **Suppose I speak in the languages of human beings and of angels. If I don't have love, I am only a loud gong or a noisy cymbal. . . . And suppose I have enough faith to move mountains. If I don't have love, I am nothing at all. Suppose I give everything I have to poor people. . . . If I don't have love, I get nothing at all. (1 Corinthians 13:1-3)**

Paul realized something important. It doesn't matter what we do, if we don't do it with love, we're just a loud noise, not helpful at all.

So, take a second and think about the ways you help your friends and family every day. What is your attitude like while you're helping them? Sure, you might be lending a hand and "obeying," but are you complaining or huffing and puffing the whole time? Would you want to be around someone like that? Whether you are unloading groceries, telling someone why you go to church or spending a Saturday morning volunteering at the food bank, **love changes the way you help people.**

◑ **WITH THAT IN MIND:**

WHAT IS SOMETHING YOU NEED TO DO TODAY THAT YOU'RE NOT TOO EXCITED ABOUT?

....

HOW CAN YOU DO THAT WITH LOVE?

....

NOW, GET TO IT. BLOW PEOPLE AWAY WITH THE WAY YOU LOVE TO HELP!

DAY 5

Who are your best friends? List them in the first column below.
What do those friends think is important or what do they like to
do? Write it out next to their names in the second column.
How do you know they like to do that? Write that down in the
third column.

BEST FRIENDS	WHAT THEY LIKE	HOW I KNOW

It's pretty easy. You know your friends and you know what they
like. After all, you've probably seen them play their favorite sport
or been to their hip-hop dance performance or noticed how they
wear bright colors every day. What they do helps you know a little
more about who they are and what they think is important.

How about you? How do you think your friends or family would
answer those same questions? Write your answers below.

MY NAME	WHAT OTHERS THINK	HOW THEY KNOW

Take a moment and call up a friend or ask a family member. Ask
them those two questions. (What do you think is important to
me? How do you know that's important to me?) Did they say what
you thought they would?

Check out what Jesus had to say about this in John 13:35:

"If you love one another, everyone will know you are my disciples."

Basically Jesus is saying that the way you act—including the way you treat others—will show people how important you think it is to follow Jesus.

Some people you know will never go to church to listen to someone talk about what it means to have a relationship with Jesus. But those same people might see the way you helped the teacher without being asked, how you were patient waiting for your turn on the video game or included someone at lunch who most people ignore. When they see you do that, they're also seeing what it means to follow Jesus. Because **when you love your friends, they will know that you love God.**

Who knows, they might ask you why you're always so nice and that would give you a great chance to tell them about Jesus!

◎ USE THE SPACE BELOW TO WRITE DOWN OR DRAW A FEW WAYS YOU CAN SHOW OTHERS THAT YOU FOLLOW JESUS BY HOW YOU LOVE THEM.

THE MOVE-IN MASH UP

Ethan studied his checklist as Emma and Lily finished loading up their backpacks. "Water?" he asked.

Lily lifted her "I Heart New York City" water bottle. "Check."

"GPS?" Ethan queried.

Emma patted her smartphone and exclaimed: "Check!"

Ethan was about to put down the list when Lily jumped in fast to add, "Hand sanitizer, detergent wipes, and surgical face masks?"

Ethan exchanged a panicked glance with Emma. They had thought Lily was loosening up, but this didn't sound promising. What would they do if she turned out to be an uptight snob, after all?

But Lily burst out giggling at the looks on their faces. "Ha! Gotcha," she crowed. "I can handle a little dirt. I'm as excited as you guys to find out what's behind The Fence!"

Ethan grinned, relieved, as they all strained to hear the distant sounds of heavy equipment. The three friends were finally setting out to explore the mysterious construction site Ethan and Emma had discovered on the other side of the woods. But as they shouldered their backpacks, they heard the sounds of a heavy truck close by.

"Wait," Ethan frowned. "What's that?"

As they rounded the corner of Ethan's house, they spotted a large moving van at the curb next door! Ethan's mother rushed to meet them, juggling a plate of cookies. "There you are!" she exclaimed. "I've told the new neighbors we'll help them unload the truck."

Ethan started to protest, but his mother was in a rush. "Emma, Lily. You can help, too. I'm sure you'd like to meet the Morenos."

Reluctantly, the three friends followed Ethan's mother across the lawn. The house next door had been empty for so long, Ethan had forgotten someone actually might buy it and move in. As they approached, he could see a dark-haired man with powerful arms handing down boxes from the moving van to several other neighbors.

"They've already got help," Ethan pointed out quickly.

Just then, a boy about their age hopped down from the back of the truck, lugging a tall lamp. "Hola!" he called out, offering a shy smile before he hurried past to get his heavy load into the house.

Mr. Morena pointed after the boy and called to them from the truck. "Mi hijo, Marco!"

Ethan stopped in his tracks, trying to understand. "Is that Spanish?" he whispered.

"Maybe he's telling us his name," Emma murmured.

Lily shook her head. "I think 'hijo' means son. So, it must be his son who's named 'Marco.'"

Ethan looked around for his mother, but she'd already disappeared into the house. Reluctantly, he led his friends up to the truck, where Mr. Moreno handed them boxes to carry. Heavy boxes.

"Muchas gracias!" Mr. Moreno exclaimed.

As they turned toward the house, Ethan adjusted his load and groaned, "What's in here, bricks?"

Ahead of them, the boy, Marco, stepped out of the house. He waved as he passed, but didn't say anything.

Emma shrugged. "I guess they don't speak any English," she said.

Ethan nodded, relieved. If Marco didn't speak English, they wouldn't have to go through the awkward steps of trying to get to know him. Adding Lily to the group had been enough!

The friends deposited their boxes in the house and returned for another load. And another one. Ethan could feel the day slipping away. "I can't believe we're stuck doing this instead of exploring," he grumbled.

"Yeah," Emma agreed. "They should have hired movers."

Lily shot them a warning glance as Marco passed again, but Ethan was past caring. "Well, they should have. And don't worry," he added, "The kid doesn't understand us anyway."

But as the friends approached the house with their next load, Marco met them on the porch. "Hello," he said. "Would you like some lunch?"

Ethan could feel his face redden. "You . . . speak English," he said at last.

"Oh, yes," Marco nodded. "My parents, not so good. But I learned at school."

Ethan tried to remember the careless, unkind things he'd said that Marco might have heard. There was no way to take them back. At last he offered, "Oh. Um, well . . . I'm Ethan."

Emma and Lily introduced themselves as well. Before Ethan could turn down the lunch offer, Lily was quick to add, "I think some lunch would be great!"

Minutes later, the friends crowded onto Marco's back porch around a dish of steaming empanadas. Ethan hung back, but Emma and Lily tried small bites.

"My mom made these," Marco told them. "They are Colombian, seasoned with lime and saffron."

Emma grinned as Lily nearly stuffed the rest of the empanada in her mouth. "I thought you didn't eat meat!" she ribbed her cousin.

"I don't!" Lily spoke through her mouthful. "But these are so good! Honest. I can't stop eating them."

Ethan crossed his arms and listened to the faint construction sounds from the woods. It seemed he was the only one who remembered they were supposed to be exploring. He cleared his throat and jumped up. "We've got some sodas at home," he said. "I'll run and get them."

Marco nodded and smiled, like they were already friends or something. Ethan frowned as he slipped through the hedge and ducked into his house through the kitchen door. "Just because he lives next door doesn't mean I have to like him!"

Ethan yanked open the fridge door, but there were no sodas inside. One more thing to annoy him. "Great," he muttered. "That means the drinks won't even be cold."

But as he turned toward the pantry where the sodas were stored, his eyes landed on the framed watercolor hanging over the counter—a passage from 1 Peter. Even though the artwork was a little cheesy, Ethan skimmed the familiar verses.

"Most of all, love one another. . . . Welcome others into your home without complaining."

Ethan sighed. Complaining was about the only thing he'd done all day. It wasn't Marco's fault that he'd messed up Ethan's plans. "I guess things are pretty upside down for him right now," Ethan considered. "With moving and everything . . ."

With new resolve, Ethan grabbed an armload of sodas and hurried back to Marco's porch to hand them out. "I hope you left me some empanadas!" he called.

Marco grinned. "There is one right here with your name on it."
As Ethan chewed, he had to admit his empanada was way better
than anything he'd eaten at a restaurant. Mrs. Moreno must have
unpacked the kitchen first thing! Through the screen door, though,
Ethan could see an ocean of boxes and pieces of furniture. It would
take days to sort it all out. Turning to Marco, Ethan suggested,
"Hey, Marco . . . I bet your bed isn't put together yet."

"It is okay," Marco said. "I will sleep on the floor."

"Maybe we could camp out in my backyard instead," Ethan
offered. "I got a really awesome tent for my birthday."

Marco hesitated. "I have never slept in a tent."

Emma jumped in, adding, "Me and Lily could come over to build
a fire and roast marshmallows, too!"

Ethan poked Emma in the shoulder. "Yeah, and Emma probably has an app on her phone to tell us what stars we can see."

Marco's eyes lit up. "Yes . . . okay! I know some really good historia de fantasmas—ghost stories."

Ethan smiled back. His summer wasn't turning out exactly like he had planned, but making a new friend was way better than losing an entire day complaining. Whatever the next few months looked like, they certainly wouldn't be boring. ■

DAY 2

What's the best sleepover you've ever been to?

Write the story of what happened at that sleepover to make it so awesome. Or if you can't think of one right now, write a few things that might make a sleepover memorable:

....

....

....

....

....

Sleepovers can be really fun. They can also be a *big* hassle—especially if the sleepover is at *your* house. You have to spend hours cleaning before everyone gets there. You sit back and watch while everyone else devours your old Valentine's candy by the handful. You inevitably get voted out of your own bed and have to sleep on the cold, hard floor. Then, you spend hours cleaning after everyone leaves. It just isn't fair!

But, like life, friendship isn't always fair. And no matter how many smelly socks you have to clean out from under your bed before a sleepover, **friends welcome each other**. First Peter 4:9 is a great verse that reminds us how we should act when our friends come over:

Welcome others into your homes without complaining.

A friendship may start at school, church, or a rec league, but really great friendships don't just happen at those places. They grow into all areas of your life, even your home. Friendships happen at birthday parties, summer camp, day trips to the amusement park, weekends at the lake, and countless hours spent in each other's homes.

God wants us to have good friends. But He knows that in order for that to happen, we have to be a good friend. That's why the Bible tells us to *welcome others into our homes without complaining.*

❷ GET TOGETHER WITH A PARENT AND PLAN TO INVITE A FRIEND OR TWO OVER TO YOUR HOME THIS WEEKEND! CREATE THE GUEST LIST. CALL YOUR FRIENDS. LET THEM DECIDE WHAT YOU WILL DO AND START GETTING READY TO WELCOME YOUR FRIENDS WITHOUT COMPLAINING!

DAY 3

Welcome.

You probably say this word a lot, as in: "You're welcome to come over and hang out!" But what does it mean to have a welcoming home?

Take this book right now and go outside.

You there? Now, open the front door and pretend that you're someone else, stepping into your house as a visitor for the very first time.

Look around. What could someone do or say that would make you feel welcome—like they're happy you're here?

Write down two things someone could do or say to make you feel welcome:

1.
....

2.
....

The Bible tells us about a couple of people who did a great job of welcoming others—not just one time, but over and over! In Acts 18, we hear about a man named Aquila and his wife Priscilla who lived in Corinth. They were actually new in town themselves, but when Paul showed up preaching and teaching about Jesus, they didn't think twice. They immediately invited him into their home and even offered him the opportunity to work with them because they were tentmakers just like he was.

Paul stayed with Aquila and Priscilla for more than a *year!* From Paul's letters, it's clear that Aquila and Priscilla continued to welcome people, because later, they invited a church to meet regularly in their home.

Once you start welcoming people, you may find yourself doing it a lot. In fact, you can **make a habit of welcoming others.**

And one of the best ways to make your friends feel welcome is to plan ahead. Yesterday, you started planning a sleepover for this weekend. Think through what you want to get ready.

Where will everyone sleep? Do you have enough sleeping bags or blankets for everyone? Maybe you could give a friend your bed while you take the floor or air mattress. And it might be a good idea to have some extra toothbrushes and toothpaste in case your friends forget theirs.

What will you do with your friends: Play games? Watch a movie? Make your *own* movie? Make sure to get everything ready so your friends know you're excited to have them, and so that they feel welcome in your house.

➋ WRITE DOWN THREE THINGS THAT YOU CAN DO AHEAD OF TIME TO MAKE YOUR FRIENDS FEEL WELCOME WHEN THEY COME:

....

....

....

DAY 4

Take a look at the list below. Draw a circle around the items that someone has shared with you.

snack	cell phone	book	movie
toy	magazine	tablet	money
chair	musical instrument	markers	CD
pencil	sports equipment	paper	hat
skateboard	video game	clothing	pen
candy	computer	backpack	bike

Now, put a box around the ones that you've shared with others. (Don't worry if some have a circle and a box—that's a good thing!)

There are usually only a couple of reasons why you might need to share something. You either needed it—like the notebook paper you didn't have for your writing assignment. Or you wanted it—like that video game you just couldn't wait to play.

Hopefully, you share things all the time, but did you know that sharing is actually part of how God wants you to treat others?

Check out what Romans 12:13 says:

> *Share with God's people who are in need. Welcome others into your homes.*

Welcoming people into your home and sharing with them is part of what it means to love others like you love yourself.

Look back at the things you put a circle around. How did you feel when people let you borrow those things?

It probably felt pretty awesome when someone let you borrow a brand-new book in your favorite series or shared a bike so you could ride around the neighborhood together. You can help others feel the same way when you **welcome others by sharing what you have.**

You will always know people who need something. They might need something fun like a skateboard or soccer ball, or it could be something pretty important like food or a place to stay. Show that you care about your friends. **Welcome others by sharing what you have.**

◑ NOW, BACK TO PLANNING THAT EPIC SLEEPOVER. EVERY GOOD PARTY NEEDS A GREAT PLAYLIST OF FUN AND UPBEAT SONGS TO KEEP THE ENERGY UP AND MAYBE EVEN MAKE EVERYONE DANCE. HOW ABOUT SHARING YOUR MUSIC AT THE PARTY? CREATE A PLAYLIST FULL OF YOUR FAVORITE SONGS. WHO KNOWS? WHEN YOU *WELCOME OTHERS BY SHARING WHAT YOU HAVE,* YOU MIGHT INTRODUCE YOUR FRIENDS TO THEIR NEXT FAVORITE BAND!

DAY 5

Have you ever been tempted to invite someone to your sleepover or birthday party just because they're popular—or because they might invite you back to one of their super cool parties?

It's true God wants you to welcome everyone, but He especially loves it when you **welcome people who can't welcome you back.**

King David didn't get everything right, but he understood how to be generous and welcome someone who couldn't help him in return. Years before, David had promised Jonathan, King Saul's son, that he would always be kind to anyone in Jonathan's family. Find a Bible or a Bible reader app and pick a version that you like. Then, go sit down at the dinner table and read 2 Samuel 9:1-13 to find out what King David did.

Still trying to figure out how to say *Mephibosheth*? You're not the only one.

Here's something pretty awesome about this story: David didn't have to do anything for Jonathan's son. In fact, he didn't even know Mephibosheth was still alive, until he asked. But David chose to welcome Mephiboseth and give him a home. David invited Mephibosheth to sit down at the king's table and eat meals with the king's family! And it changed Mephibosheth's life forever.

Ask yourself right now: is there someone you could invite to your sleepover who probably won't invite you back or make you look cool? If someone comes to mind, ask your parents about adding them to the invite list.

❂ LIKE DAVID, YOU'VE ALREADY INVITED SOME FRIENDS TO COME AND HAVE A MEAL WITH YOU—WHETHER THAT'S DINNER, A MIDNIGHT SNACK, OR BREAKFAST! TAKE A FEW MINUTES AND WRITE DOWN WHAT YOU WANT TO SERVE YOUR FRIENDS TO EAT RIGHT HERE AT THIS TABLE. DON'T FORGET THE POPCORN FOR A MOVIE OR MAYBE PANCAKE POPS FOR BREAKFAST!

....

....

....

FRIENDS

TEACH EACH OTHER

THE
TREE
HOUSE
CHALLENGE

Marco paused briefly, picking up a fallen branch to use as a sturdy walking stick. Then he hurried to catch up with Ethan, who led the way through the woods, whistling. Emma skipped along behind with Lily. All four friends tuned their ears to hear the sounds of construction equipment that filtered through the trees.

"Amigos," Marco asked. "That noise. It is where we go?"

Emma nearly bubbled over with excitement as she adjusted her backpack. "That's where we go next," she explained. "After we build our fort."

"Yeah," Ethan nodded. "We're ready to launch our expedition. So, we need a tree fort."

"Mission headquarters," Emma clarified.

Soon, the group of friends arrived beneath a huge oak tree. Sunlight filtered through its wide, leafy branches. Ethan dropped his heavy pack in between the roots. "This is it!" he exclaimed.

Emma, too, dropped her backpack and began unzipping it. "Hope you guys packed all the most important stuff for our fort!"

Marco nodded as he reached for his backpack. His father built houses, so he knew all the special things any new construction needed. He had carefully considered what the tree house would require. "I have something muy importante—" he began. "Something very important."

Before Marco could even unzip his bag, though, Ethan upended his own pack. Several thick coils dropped out. "The most important thing is: rope!"

Emma frowned. "What's that for?"

Ethan began unwrapping the thick cords. "There's enough here to knot a forty-foot rope ladder," he said proudly.

"Forty feet?!" Emma's jaw dropped. "We can't build our fort that high up. Plus, it'll take all day just to make the ladder."

"Not if you all help," Ethan pointed out.

"I don't know how to do knots," Emma declared. "Anyhow, I have to get us online."

Marco sighed. His friends were going about this all wrong, but he wasn't sure they would listen to him. After all, he was new to the neighborhood.

Emma had already opened up her bag to reveal a nest of wires and gadgets. Lily raised an eyebrow. "Earth to Emma. Where are you planning to plug in?"

"It's all solar powered!" Emma crowed. "I need to install a charging station for our walkies, plus a camera to monitor the trail when we're up in the tree. Oh, and flood lights."

Lily swished her ponytail again. "You guys have totally missed the most important thing."

Marco nodded, relieved. "Si, si. Yes, I have. . . ."

But before Marco could reveal the contents of his backpack, Lily began yanking yards and yards of shimmering, brightly-painted fabric from her backpack. "The most important thing is . . . a sun screen!"

Marco sighed. Emma raised an eyebrow and asked, "Is that silk?"

"I made it in this totally awesome screen printing class I took," Lily explained. "It'll protect us from the sun."

"We have leaves, in case you didn't notice," Ethan scoffed.

"Seriously, people!" Lily chided. "Sunburn is, like, toxic. Plus, putting this up will give our headquarters the coolest vibe ever! And I saw these quartz rocks along the trail we could use to decorate."

"Decorate?!" Ethan groaned.

Marco tried to break in once again, but Lily spoke over him. "We're supposed to work together, right? That's the most important thing."

This tree house was going to be a disaster! Marco finally gave up worrying whether the others would listen to him and shouted, "The most important thing!"

Everyone stopped to stare at Marco. He took a deep breath. "The most important thing . . . it is that we all have something to share. There is a Bible verse . . . " Marco's mind went blank. He'd learned the verse in Spanish, from his grandmother, and he was too nervous right now to get the English translation right. "Uh . . . estan capacitados para—"

Lily blinked. "My Spanish goes about as far as gracias?"

Marco struggled to find the words. "I learned it in Spanish, so that is what keeps coming to my mind. Instruir . . . that is, to teach. . . . "

Emma grabbed her phone and quickly launched an app. "Hey!" she exclaimed. "You can just say it into here."

She held out the mic end to Marco, who carefully repeated the verse in Spanish. Then Emma tapped the translator button. The phone repeated back to them in halting English: "My brothers and sisters, I am sure that you are full of goodness. What you know is complete. You are able to teach one another."

Marco nodded, excited. "Si! Yes, that is it. All of us have something to teach the others."

Lily glanced up the length of the soaring tree trunk. "Well, we totally do need Ethan to show us how to build a ladder. . . . "

"And Emma can teach us all how to set up her wires and stuff, Ethan added. "I mean, what's a secret mission without tech support?"

Emma ran her hands over the silky fabric Lily had brought. "We don't *need* to decorate. But our fort will be way more awesome if Lily shows us how to make it look cool."

They all turned to Marco, who was grinning broadly. They still hadn't figured it out! Ethan punched Marco in the shoulder. "And Marco showed us we've got to teach each other rather than just doing it our own way. Right?"

"There is something else," Marco told them. "Muy importante."

Reaching into his pack, he pulled out two items and displayed them for his friends: a hammer and a box of nails. "Mi padre, he is a contractor. A builder. You cannot build anything until you have a foundation."

The others stared at Marco. He waved up toward the branches. "Where did you think we would stand in the tree? Or sit?"

The other three friends stared at each other for a moment, mouths hanging open. Then they all burst out laughing.

"I guess we were just going to float!" Lily giggled.

"Or hop from branch to branch like squirrels," Emma added.

Marco began dragging a straight, fallen branch from the brush. "We will carry these up, with rope, like so, then lay them across and nail them down." He gestured to demonstrate exactly how they could lay a solid foundation.

Ethan smiled ruefully. "Last time I used a hammer, I hammered my thumb!" he confessed.

"Do not worry," Marco encouraged. "I will show you!"

Under Marco's guidance, the friends began selecting sturdy branches. It might take a few extra days, but they were confident each one of them had something important to share. There was no question the completed fort would be amazing—the perfect launch point for their mission. ∎

DAY 2

Who taught you how to . . .

READ?...

WRITE?...

SWIM?...

RIDE A BIKE?...

No one is born knowing everything they need to know to get through life. It's up to people around us—our parents, teachers, coaches, friends—to teach us along the way. And you know what? It's up to you to teach others, too. Because **friends teach each other.**

Romans 15:14 says:

> *My brothers and sisters, I am sure that you are full of goodness. What you know is complete. You are able to teach one another.*

You may not know how to teach your little cousin to ride a bike. You probably wouldn't know where to begin to teach someone how to read. But there are some things you could teach someone. Maybe you are really great at a sport. Maybe you know how to draw or paint really well. Maybe you are the only person you know who has gotten to the highest level of your favorite video game. Whatever it is, we all have a gift—a talent—and we are wired to share with others. We are wired to teach!

Take a minute to write three skills you have that you could teach someone else:

1. ....

2. ....

3. ....

Sharing those skills is a big part of friendship. But friends don't just teach each other how to karate chop a concrete block or how to pull off a wheelie on their bikes. **Friends teach each other** about God, too. That's right. When you hear a cool story or learn something new about God, it's important to share it with your friends!

But it's hard to teach others about God before you have thought through what you know about Him and who you think He is. So, take some time and write down what you know about God so far.

✪ WRITE THREE WORDS TO DESCRIBE GOD:

1. ....

2. ....

3. ....

✪ WRITE ABOUT A TIME GOD DID SOMETHING COOL IN YOUR LIFE:

....

....

....

✪ WRITE ONE THING GOD HAS TAUGHT YOU:

....

....

....

DAY 3

Everyone follows someone—at church, at school, and in other activities. Your mom or dad follows a boss at work. Your friend may follow the instructions from a baseball coach. Some people may follow whatever their friends say.

Write down two adults or older kids you're following.

....

....

Now think about the kinds of things these people teach you—whether it's a sport, long division, or what to do when a friend says something mean to you.

Write down something you've learned from one of those people this month.

....

....

Did you know it's easy to start acting and thinking like the people you follow? Some things they teach you on purpose, and some things you learn simply from hanging out with them. That's why it's important to make sure you are following the right people— wise people. Because **when you learn from wise people, you have wisdom to share with others.**

One of the most amazing guys in the Old Testament was a man named Elijah—a wise prophet who listened to God and spoke God's words to the people and to powerful kings! It was a hard, lonely job, and Elijah probably wondered who on earth would be able to take over when he was finished.

That's where a young man named Elisha comes in. God told Elijah to pick Elisha as an assistant. Elisha would travel with Elijah everywhere and watch him at work. Elijah did just as God told him and chose Elisha to be the next prophet. Elisha followed Elijah around for some time, watching how he lived—Elisha even witnessed Elijah confront a powerful king! Then, God decided it was time to bring Elijah home. The story involves a wide, roaring river!

Pick up a Bible or open a Bible reader app and choose a version you like. Then, go find some water. Maybe you've got a creek nearby, or a neighborhood pool or pond. Or maybe you can run the hose and set up the Slip'N Slide in the backyard.

(If nothing else, fill up the bathtub or sit next to a roaring shower!)

❍ SIT DOWN AND READ 1 KINGS 19:19-21 AND 2 KINGS 2:1-15 BESIDE THE WATER. HOW DO YOU THINK ELISHA WOULD HAVE FELT WHEN HE SAW ELIJAH PART WATER? WHAT DO YOU THINK ELISHA LEARNED? WRITE DOWN ONE OR TWO THOUGHTS IN THE SPACE BELOW. AND REMEMBER, JUST LIKE ELISHA LEARNED FROM THE WISE OLD PROPHET, ELIJAH: *WHEN YOU LEARN FROM WISE PEOPLE, YOU HAVE WISDOM TO SHARE WITH OTHERS.*

DAY 4

Who are your friends? Draw a quick sketch of four of your friends or write their names in the boxes below.

Now, take a moment to think about a few of the reasons you are friends with those people. Write those reasons here:

....

....

....

Your friends probably like the same things you do or are in your class at school or on your sports team. Maybe they're hilarious or just really nice.

Whatever the specific reasons, you're friends with them simply because you like hanging out together.

Now ask yourself this: Have any of the people you sketched above ever taught you anything?

Even something small like how to beat that Xbox® game, tell a joke, or get away with not doing your homework every night? (Not that *your* friends would *ever* do that last one.)

Did you know that when it comes to learning, your friends play a big part?

Check out what King Solomon, one of the wisest men who ever lived, wrote down in Proverbs 13:20 about the people we hang out with:

Anyone who walks with wise people grows wise. But a companion of foolish people suffers harm.

You're pretty smart yourself, so you probably know what a fool is. But just in case you don't, a fool is basically a person who knows the right thing to do but chooses not to do it. They know the right thing to do is not to climb on the roof of their house, yet they choose to climb up and jump off with an umbrella (Mary-Poppins-style) anyway.

Yeah, not so smart, huh? Think about it: What happens if you hang out with fools?

Exactly. Nothing good can come from that.

So, take a look at those four pictures you drew or names you wrote down. On a scale of 1 to 5 (5 being super wise and 1 being foolish), how wise are your friends? Be honest.

❸ HOPEFULLY, YOU'RE HANGING OUT WITH SOME OF THE WISEST PEOPLE YOU KNOW. IF NOT, TRY BUMPING THE "FOOLS" ON YOUR FRIEND LIST AND REPLACING THEM WITH SOMEONE A LITTLE WISER. BECAUSE IF YOU WANT TO BE A WISE FRIEND YOURSELF, YOU NEED TO HANG OUT WITH PEOPLE WHO TEACH YOU HOW TO BE WISE.

DAY 5

What's your favorite movie? How many times have you watched it? Like a *million*?

If asked, you could probably give every last detail of that story—spoiler alerts and all.

Some stories are just memorable. Whether it's the one about a sister who risks everything to melt her frozen world or the one about a team of superheroes joining together to save the world from an alien invasion, stories make you think about what you would do in similar situations. Sometimes stories can even cause you to change the way you think.

What about your own story? Do you have a life-changing story—one that everyone would want to hear? Well, if you know Jesus, you have a great story, one full of hope and joy—one worth telling.

But are you ready to tell it?

Peter, one of Jesus' closest friends, wrote a letter to some other followers of Jesus. He told them this:

> *Always be ready to give an answer to anyone who asks you about the hope you have. Be ready to give the reason for it. But do it gently and with respect. (1 Peter 3:15b)*

If you don't know your story—the story of how you first heard about Jesus and what He has done in your life—you're not ready. Take a few minutes to answer these questions so you can be ready to teach your friends about Jesus and the amazing story God is telling through your life.

When and how did you first hear about God's big story?

....

....

When did you believe in Jesus?

....

....

How has God changed your life since then?

....

....

How has God answered your prayers?

....

....

What has God taught you?

....

....

❥   AND YOU KNOW WHAT? THESE COULD BE SOME GREAT
QUESTIONS TO ASK YOUR FRIENDS AND FAMILY, TOO! YOU
NEVER KNOW WHAT YOU MIGHT LEARN ABOUT GOD WHEN
YOU TALK WITH OTHERS ABOUT HIM.

THE BIRTHDAY EMERGENCY

When Emma and Lily cut through the hedge into the backyard next door, they found Ethan and Marco already seated around the remains of last night's campfire.

Ethan grinned as he handed half his granola bar to Marco. "You're late!" he announced, as if he'd just convicted them of a crime.

"Nope," Emma declared. "You guys are just early. It's exactly 9 a.m."

Emma waved her smartphone showing the time as proof. She plopped down on a split log and whipped out a clipboard with a detailed list.

Marco peered at it. "Why do we need that?"

"We're planning our mission!" Emma announced. Though the sky was brilliant blue now, a wild storm had whipped through during the night. Emma didn't mind thunder, but she'd woken up early anyway and used the time to make a careful list of everything the friends might need to take care of today.

Lily shook her head, making her squiggly silver earrings dance in the sunlight. "You should have heard her at breakfast. She has, like, the entire day scheduled."

"First, we check in at mission headquarters," Emma began.

"Oh, yes. Our tree fort!" Marco exclaimed.

"Have to see if the storm last night did any damage," Ethan agreed.

"Exactly!" Emma beamed, glad to see that everyone was on board. "We'll do any necessary repairs and gather provisions from our stock. Then we'll circle through the woods and approach the fence from the north instead of the west, since the ground by the creek will be all muddy."

Her friends nodded. It was high time they finally discovered what was being built behind the 12-foot fence that stretched out on the other side of the woods.

"Do we try to climb it?" Lily asked.

"I think we should start by analyzing the construction sounds," Emma decided. "If we know the kind of equipment being used, Marco can tell us what kind of building site it is. We'll record the sounds and then search online to match them up with the right machinery!"

Emma flashed her smartphone again to demonstrate how the mic worked. But Lily froze as she noticed the display. "What's that?" she asked, panic in her voice.

Emma glanced at the phone. "You mean my screensaver? Just date and time—"

"June 19!" Lily moaned. She popped up off her log seat and began pacing.

The others stared at her. "Yeah? So?" Emma asked.

"It's my mom's birthday!" Lily wailed.

Emma nodded. "Aunt Jill," she said.

Lily's face crumpled. "I didn't even get her anything."

Marco reached over and tapped Emma's phone. "Call her, amiga," he suggested kindly.

"No!" Lily said. "I need to do something extra special. Things aren't . . . good right now. At home."

Emma wanted to ask exactly what the trouble was between Aunt Jill and Uncle Ted. After all, their problems were the reason Lily was staying with Emma for the summer. But the boys jumped in before Emma could say a word.

"You could make her something," Ethan suggested. "Like that tent thing you painted for the fort!"

Lily shook her head. "There's, like, no time to ship it."

"You should have thought ahead," Emma pointed out.

"I didn't, okay?!" Lily said sharply.

Marco was still considering. "You could make for her . . . a video."

Lily lit up. "Oh, that's good! She likes to see me dance. I do jazz. And classical. Or I could do hip hop." Lily demonstrated each step, moving seamlessly from one to the other. The boys applauded.

"We could all sing!" Marco offered.

"English *and* Spanish!" Ethan grinned.

Marcos began a round of "Happy Birthday" in Spanish. "Feliz Cumpleaños a ti. . . . "

Within moments, the guys had formed a sort of boy band, while Lily leapt and twisted across the lawn. Emma frowned and whacked her clipboard against her split log seat.

"Hey!" she shouted.

They all stopped, briefly, to look at her.

"Guys! This could take all day!"

"But that's okay," Lily said. "I mean, as long as we can edit and send it by bedtime."

"We must take time to practice," Marco added. "To do it well!"

"Emma, you could sing backup!" Lily invited.

Emma stared at the carefully planned mission on her clipboard. They'd been working toward this for so long. And now, once again, they would miss their chance to explore. Emma cleared her throat. "I meant, we don't have time for this. *I* don't have time for it. I'm gonna go rewire our walkie-talkies."

She stalked away without even turning to see whether her friends were watching. At home, she hurried straight up to her room and yanked the door open, slamming it against the wall. She thumped down hard on her bed.

"It's not fair!" she muttered. "We lose the whole day 'cause Lily didn't plan ahead."

Emma started to pick up one of the walkie-talkies on her nightstand, but a box on Lily's bed drew her attention. The cardboard flaps stood open, revealing an odd assortment of items. Curious, Emma stepped over to look. She spotted a dozen packs of watermelon mint gum. Artsy bangles. Tubes of fabric paint. A puffy stuffed octopus. And a silver chain with imprinted pieces of plastic strung on it.

"Guitar picks?" Emma wondered aloud.

Without thinking, she picked up the chain—about the length of a necklace. It appeared each guitar pick was printed with a different Bible verse about how to treat others. Emma read the first one. "Don't be proud at all. . . . Be patient. Put up with one another in love."

Emma frowned. Images of slamming the clipboard on the log and storming away flooded her memory. She hadn't shown any patience. But didn't someone have to think ahead?

"Hey!" Lily's voice rang out, and Emma snapped to attention. She glanced up to see Lily standing in the doorway, arms crossed, fire in her eyes.

"That's mine!" Lily snapped.

"It was just lying here, okay!" Emma said defensively. But then she felt the anger slipping away. "Look, I'm sorry."

Lily softened, too. She came and sat down on the edge of the bed beside Emma. "My grandpa sent it. The whole box. He put my favorite stuff in it to cheer me up."

Emma nodded. She carefully laid the chain and guitar picks in Lily's outstretched hand. "What are these?"

"I guess . . . " Lily began. "I guess Grandpa George knew I might have trouble making friends in a new place. He thought I might need some reminders about what it means to be a good friend."

"Yeah. I, um . . . sort of need reminders, too," Emma confessed.

Lily nodded, and the girls sat in silence for a moment. Then Emma jumped up, grabbing her flip camera off the desk. "Hey," she announced. "We've got to get moving if you want me to tape this video for Aunt Jill!"

Laughing, the two cousins headed back outside. Emma knew that, for today, her most important mission was simply being there for her friend. Even if everything else had to wait. ■

DAY 2

House training a puppy.
Saving up for a new gaming system.
Waiting in line at Hollywood Studios®.

Some things take patience. But most things that take patience are worth it in the end. Knowing you won't step in a puddle of puppy pee on the way to the fridge. The hours of entertainment provided by your brand new PlayStation®. The once-in-a-lifetime feeling of being dropped from "The Tower of Terror."

Totally worth it.

Take a minute and write down three things you have to do this week that might take a little patience, but are worth it:

1. ....

2. ....

3. ....

Ephesians 4:2 tells us:

> *Don't be proud at all. Be completely gentle. Be patient. Put up with one another in love.*

Did you catch that? Not only is it worth it to be patient for things we want, but the Bible tells us to be patient with people around us. This verse reminds us that **friends are patient with each other.**

Just like you might have to wait in line before you can ride an awesome ride, you may have to wait for your friend to clean his room before you can show him your new bike. And, just like the "Tower of Terror," friendship is *totally* worth it in the end. Maybe you and your friend are finally on your way to see the newest superhero movie. You don't want to miss a second—not even the part when they tell you to silence your cell phones—but your friend can't decide which type of candy he wants! Or maybe you invited a friend to the beach with your family. All you want to do is ride the waves on your boogie board, but your friend is all about building an entire sand village.

Being patient with one another—putting up with one another in love—could mean spending a little extra time doing what someone else wants to do. Friendship is more important than seeing the previews before your movie or a couple hours surfing the waves.

❷ CHECK OUT THESE THREE SCENARIOS. UNDERNEATH EACH ONE, WRITE HOW YOU COULD BE A GOOD FRIEND BY BEING PATIENT!

1.   You spent the night at your friend's house and are eager to get ooey-gooey donuts from the new local bakery for breakfast. But you have to wait for your friend's favorite shirt to finish drying before you can leave.

....

....

2.   You are paired with your best friend on a project at school. You like getting your schoolwork out of the way so you can enjoy your stress-free weekends. But your friend is a wait-'til-the-last-minute kind of person.

....

....

3.   You let your friend borrow your new game for the weekend, but when Monday rolls around, they forgot it at home.

....

....

DAY 3

In the box below, write about the last time you got angry and went crazy. Maybe you got out in the bottom of the ninth, a friend said something mean about you, or your mom asked you to clean up the "presents" your dog left in the yard.

How'd that make you feel? What happened? Did getting angry help the situation?

In the story you just wrote, did anything good happen as a result of getting angry?

Probably not, huh?

When you get angry and lose your cool, there's a good chance that someone will get hurt in the process.

Take a look at what King Solomon wrote in the book of Proverbs:

A man who burns with anger stirs up fights. But a person who is patient calms things down. (Proverbs 15:18)

Anger only causes problems. On the other hand, when you're patient you get a chance to calm down and choose your words wisely. Then, you might be able to understand what is really happening. See, **when you are patient with others, you can make peace.**

But you don't always know that anger is creeping around the corner. A friend can say something mean. You can get a bad grade on a test. Or your sister eats the last of your favorite cereal for breakfast. And in an instant, you're about to go crazy!

There's a better way. Before you say anything, go punch a pillow, or count backwards from 20. Or better yet, memorize the Bible verse above and say it out loud or in your head a few times.

> *A person who is patient calms things down.*
> *A person who is patient calms things down.*
> *A person who is patient calms things down.*
> *(Proverbs 15:18b)*

Or even better, ask God to give you patience. He can do that because He can change your attitude. And when you feel yourself getting frustrated with your friends, ask yourself: "Will this calm things down? Will this make peace?" Because when you are patient with others, you can make peace.

❷ GIVEN THE CHOICE BETWEEN ANGER AND PATIENCE, IT'S A NO BRAINER: PATIENCE WINS EVERY TIME.

DAY 4

Go find a mirror. Maybe in your room or the bathroom. Even the back of a spoon could work for this.

Now, make the angriest face you can. No smiling. No laughing. Just you and your angry face. Scrunch your nose. Grit your teeth. Squint your eyes.

Get *angry!*

What do you see? Not your prettiest face, huh?

Know what? That might be how others see you when you get frustrated, mad, and *angry!*

Know what else? The Bible talks a lot about getting angry. In fact, it must have been a pretty big issue because God mentions it so often. Check it out; this is a passage from a book of the Bible called James.

> *My dear brothers and sisters, pay attention to what I say. Everyone should be quick to listen. But they should be slow to speak. They should be slow to get angry. (James 1:19)*

Whoa. That's a lot in one verse. Let's break it all down. God is telling us to be three things:

Quick to listen. When you're frustrated with someone, listening to their side of the story is the last thing you want to do. But the Bible says it should be the first thing we think about when we're not getting along with each other.

Slow to speak. How many times have you said something without thinking? Sometimes you can get so frustrated you just say whatever pops into your head. The problem is, when you're frustrated, hurtful words are usually what pop into your head.

Slow to get angry. How often do you "hit the pause button" on how you're feeling? It's a really hard thing to do. But taking a moment to think about why you're getting angry might help you avoid a messy argument with your friends.

Doing all three of those things takes a lot of patience. At some point, one of your friends will do something to get on your nerves. It's just gonna happen. But if you show patience and listen—if you **pause before you get angry**—you might understand their side of the story and avoid an argument altogether.

So, head back to that mirror. (Or go grab that spoon!) This time, make the biggest smile ever—like a huge, squinty-eyed, all-your-teeth kind of smile!

That's better than your angry face, isn't it?

◑ NEXT TIME YOU'RE IN A FRUSTRATING SITUATION, PAUSE BEFORE YOU GET ANGRY. THINK ABOUT THE DIFFERENCE BETWEEN YOUR ANGRY FACE AND YOUR HAPPY FACE. WHICH FACE WOULD YOU RATHER SEE? THEN, PRACTICE BEING . . .

1. **Quick to listen.**
2. **Slow to speak.**
3. **Slow to get angry.**

DAY 5

Look at the sentence below and write down the first word that pops into your head when you read it.

Love is ....

There are lots of words you could have written in that blank. I bet you can think of three more right now.

....

....

....

There are lots of ways to define the word love, because there are lots of ways people show love to each other.

Did you know there is a "love" chapter in the Bible? There is. It's 1 Corinthians 13. In that chapter, most of the verses are dedicated to the idea of how people should love one another. One of those words is the idea we're focusing on this week.

Check it out:

Love is patient. (1 Corinthians 13:4a)

Now, you may be asking yourself, "How is love patient?"

Think about it.

When your mom waits for you to finish reading that chapter before she asks you to come to the dinner table . . .

When your friends let you play that one-player game on their Xbox One® while they just sit on the couch . . .

When you take the time to read your little brother or sister a book before going outside to play with your friends . . .

That's patience; that's showing love.

A few weeks ago, we talked about how important it is to show your friends love. And if you want to know a little secret about this book, you probably could have stopped there. That is, if you truly, 100 percent, without-a-doubt, understand what it means to love your friends. But love is a vague and unclear word. Love is complicated and hard to define. That's what all the rest of these weeks are about—helping you understand a bit more clearly how to love your friends. And one of the ways to show love is to be patient with your friends.

❂ USING THE WORD *PATIENCE* BELOW, WRITE A FEW WAYS YOU CAN SHOW LOVE BY THE WAY YOU ARE PATIENT WITH YOUR FRIENDS.

P...

A...

T...

I...

E...

N...

C...

E...

FRiENDS

SERVE EACH OTHER.

THE
PIRATE
DIRECTOR

Just yesterday, Ethan, Emma, Lily and Marco had finally made it all the way to the mysterious, high fence that stood on the other side of the woods! They had heard the construction sounds inside, but were unable to figure out what lay beyond. It was a big disappointment.

"We've got to scale it," Ethan decided. "Pretty sure I could do that with the right climbing gear."

"Then you can attach the rope ladder for the rest of us!" Emma added. "We should upgrade our walkie-talkies, though. We'll need hands-free."

"Si, si!" Marco applauded.

"Let's do it!" Lily agreed.

But their parents weren't eager to pay for expensive gear. "I trust you kids to be careful out in the woods," Ethan's mother said. "But if you want fancy equipment, you're going to have to earn the money to pay for it."

The four friends gathered in their tree fort to plan. "Lemonade stand?" Ethan offered.

"We could bake cookies to sell," Emma suggested.

"Or wash cars . . . " Marco added.

Lily yawned and stretched over in a backbend. Her silver chain necklace, strung with guitar picks, fell up around her ears. "Boooooooring!" she declared.

"You have something better?" Ethan challenged. He thought a lemonade stand was pretty good. Sure, it wasn't the most creative idea in the world, but he had made good money last time he tried it in third grade.

"Yeah!" Lily shot back. "That video we did for my mom turned out so well. I think we should, like, hire ourselves out to do parties. You know, shoot a fun video of the birthday kid. Organize dance games. Decorate cake pops?"

The others had to admit it was a pretty great idea. Even Ethan gave in. "I bet Mom will let me use our garage as a studio," he said.

Marco nodded. "And I can draw pictures for a poster."

"And fliers!" Emma agreed. "That's perfect. I'll get mom to post it on the neighborhood Facebook page, too."

The friends handed out fliers and landed their first client within hours. Everyone grouped around Ethan as he took the phone call. When he got off the line, he proudly announced, "Gavin Luce is turning six. His mom wants us to do a pirate party. On Saturday!"

"How do we begin, amigos?" Marco asked.

Ethan opened up a folding director's chair and grandly took a seat. "We should create a pirate set and film Gavin as a Pirate Captain on the high seas! Marco, go get branches and stuff for a desert island. Lily, put up some kind of backdrop. There's leftover paint in that corner you can use to make a pirate ship. Emma, we need better lighting. Get those lamps from your family room. And an extension cord."

Emma stared him down, arms crossed. "What will *you* be doing while the rest of us are working hard?"

Ethan settled back into his chair and took a long drink of his ice-cold soda. "*I* will be working on the script."

Lily raised an eyebrow. "You don't even have paper," she pointed out.

Ethan rolled his eyes. "I'm writing in my head." He reached for a bag of chips and began munching thoughtfully.

With a few dark looks at Ethan, the others scattered to complete their tasks. By lunchtime, the garage was beginning to look a little bit like a tropical island. But there was a long way to go.

"Emma," Ethan commanded. "You should haul in some sand from that old sandbox in your back yard. We need to move it, people!"

"We're trying, okay?" Emma retorted.

"I've completely plotted out the script," Ethan declared. "You should be done by now!"

"Well, I still have to paint the mast," Lily pointed out. "And the sails."

Ethan shrugged. "Then get Marco to help. Oh, and reach up on that shelf and get me that director's cap."

"Quit bossing us around!" Emma glared at him.

Lily put her hand on Emma's shoulder. "It's okay. I'll get it."

But as Lily reached up, her necklace chain snagged on the sharp corner of the metal shelving. It snapped, sending plastic guitar picks flying everywhere. "Oh, no!" she cried.

Marco jumped in quickly. "I will help!" he said as he scrambled across the floor, corralling picks.

Lily and Emma joined as Ethan groaned. "Great. At this rate, you'll never finish!" Reluctantly, he reached down to nab one of the picks that had landed beside his chair. He frowned as he saw the words printed on it.

"What are these?" he asked.

"Reminders," Lily said. "From my Grandpa."

Ethan frowned as he read the words. "Serve one another in love."

"They're Bible verses," Lily explained. "Grandpa thought I might have a hard time making friends this summer. Being in a new place and all."

Ethan swallowed as he stared at the guitar pick. He could feel the heat rising in his face. After all, he'd spent the whole day ordering around his friends. He wasn't serving anyone but himself.

Sighing, he confessed, "You're already a good friend. All of you. Better than I've been today."

"Yeah. No kidding!" Lily commented. Then she laughed. "I'm joking, okay? You just got a little carried away."

Ethan's mother poked her head into the garage. "Would you kids like some lunch?"

Everyone moved toward the door, but Ethan jumped up. "No! Stop," he ordered. "You guys take a break. I'll get lunch and bring it in here for you."

Ethan returned with sandwiches for each of his friends. "Turkey and olives for Emma. . . . "

Marco peered at the sandwich. "That is . . . ugh!"

"Yeah!" Ethan grinned. "But it's what she's eaten since kindergarten. Marco, you like ham and Swiss, right?" He handed Marco a sandwich and then turned to give the last one to Lily. "PB and J, no meat."

As the friends finished up their lunch break, Ethan slapped the director's cap on his head and crossed his arms. "Now, here's what we're going to do!" he announced.

His friends exchanged worried glances, but Ethan grinned. "Gotcha, didn't I? Right now, *I* am going to help Lily finish up the ship. And then *I* am hauling that sand from your backyard, Emma."

Laughing, the friends returned to work. Ethan had to admit that it all went a lot more smoothly . . . now that he was looking out for his friends rather than just himself. ■

DAY 2

Wait!

Before you start today's devotion, take a spin around your house. See if anyone needs help with something. Is there anything you see that would help out a parent? A brother or sister? A pet? What are you waiting for? Get going!

Are you done? Great! Take a few minutes and write out how you were able to serve your family just now:

....

....

....

In Galatians 5:13b, the Bible tells us to:

Serve one another in love.

We all need a little help sometimes, but it's not just your family that needs to be served. **Friends serve each other, too.** That's right, in order to be a good friend, it's important to serve each other and help out whenever someone needs you!

But let's check out that verse from Galatians one more time: "Serve one another *in love*." Did you catch those last two words? The Bible doesn't just tell us to serve each other. It tells us to serve each other in *love*. (There's that mushy-gushy word again.) No, it doesn't mean you have to be "in love" with your friends. It is simply pointing out the difference between huffing, puffing and slapping your feet against the pavement while helping your friend walk his neighbor's dogs . . . and eagerly grabbing the leashes with a great big smile, letting your friend know there's nothing in the world you'd rather be doing.

Serving each other is all about attitude. When you do something for someone cheerfully and eagerly, you show your love. Not sure if you can tell the difference between serving "in love" and serving without love? Check out the drawings below. Circle the ones that show friends serving each other in love. Put a big "X" through the ones that show friends serving without love.

❂ GREAT JOB! I BET THOSE WERE EASIER THAN YOU THOUGHT. NOW THAT YOU HAVE A PRETTY GOOD CLUE ABOUT WHAT SERVING ONE ANOTHER IN LOVE MEANS, GET TO IT! KEEP YOUR EYES OPEN FOR WAYS YOU CAN SERVE YOUR FRIENDS . . . WITH A SMILE ON YOUR FACE!

DAY 3

Field trip! Take this book outside. Walk away from your house or building. Now, turn around and look up—at the roof.

Pretty high up, huh? How hard do you think it would be to climb up there?

Okay, now imagine that you and three of your friends have to somehow carry another friend all the way up there.

And now, imagine that not only have you and your friends hauled another friend up there, but now you have to break through the roof! This really happened in the Bible! It may sound wild but **friends do what it takes to serve their friends**. Your friends have probably never asked you to break through someone's roof before. (And if they do, you may want to think twice about exactly why they need you to do it!) But when you have a friend in need, you do what it takes! And in Luke 5:17-26, there's a story of a few friends willing to do whatever it took to serve their friend.

Jesus had been teaching and healing so many people that *huge* crowds followed Him, pressing in everywhere He went. If Jesus was talking inside someone's living room, not only would the whole house be packed, but there would be people filling the yard and the street, too!

Four guys had a friend who couldn't walk. They knew Jesus could heal their friend, but with the crowd so crazy, there was no way they'd ever make it inside the front door or anywhere close to Jesus. So, they decided to think outside the box. *Above* the box, actually.

◎ FIND A BIBLE OR A BIBLE READER APP. NOW, YOU PROBABLY CAN'T GET UP ON YOUR ROOF, BUT FIND THE HIGHEST PLACE YOU CAN—LIKE A TREE HOUSE, BALCONY, OR THE TOP FLOOR OF YOUR HOUSE—AND SIT THERE TO READ LUKE 5:17-26. LOOK FOR THE INCREDIBLE WAY IN WHICH THESE GUYS SHOWED HOW FRIENDS DO WHAT IT TAKES TO SERVE THEIR FRIENDS.

DAY 4

Have you ever won a trophy?

Have you ever *wanted* to win a trophy? Or a medal? Or some ginormous thing that would show the world how awesome you are?

Take a minute and draw the trophy you'd want to get.

Why do you think people want trophies and medals?

It feels good to be first. The first one to cross the finish line. The first one in line for the newest video game. The first one to get a slice of birthday cake.

It feels good to be recognized as the best or chosen as important enough to be first. If you've ever felt like that, you know how important it is for others to experience that, too. You know how important it is to **serve your friends by putting them first.**

Check out what Romans 12:10 says:

Love each other deeply. Honor others more than yourselves.

Romans chapter 12 is all about putting the love God shows us into action. One of the ways you can do that is by honoring your friends and letting them see how valuable they really are. And a great way to show someone how valuable and important they are is to **put them first.**

Look back at that trophy you drew for yourself. The cool thing is, you don't need to give your friends trophies to show them honor and put them first. Trophies are great and all, but most people would rather have your friendship than a trophy. Show them how much they mean to you by serving them, honoring them, and putting them first.

There are all sorts of ways you can do this. You can let them pick what movie to watch or what game to play. You could give them first-dibs on the LEGO bricks. You can let them go ahead of you in line at the ice cream shop—you could even pay for their ice cream.

❂ WRITE DOWN A FEW SPECIFIC WAYS THAT YOU CAN SERVE *YOUR* FRIENDS BY PUTTING THEM FIRST:

1 ....

2 ....

3 ....

4 ....

5 ....

DAY 5

Ever heard of the television show *Dirty Jobs*?

While lots of people work in tidy, air-conditioned offices, there are still some pretty messy jobs that someone's got to do. *Dirty Jobs* introduces some incredibly icky work, like:

- Collecting roadkill
- Emptying Porta-Potties
- Spreading hot tar on roofs
- Turning trash into electricity
- Making flower pots from cow manure

Yuck! Maybe you'll never be a pig farmer or collect owl vomit, but you will have opportunities to help out a friend by getting messy or doing something difficult for them. In fact, **sometimes serving means doing the dirty work.**

- Maybe one of your friends is moving, and you help carry the big, awkward boxes.
- Maybe your friend can't play video games until their super messy room is clean, and you volunteer to help.
- Maybe your friend's mom just made you both some amazing lasagna, and after dinner you jump in, rinsing all the dishes and putting them in the dishwasher.

WRITE DOWN TWO "DIRTY JOBS" YOU MIGHT BE ABLE TO HELP A FRIEND WITH.

....

....

◑ NOW FIND A BIBLE OR BIBLE READER APP AND OPEN UP TO THE TIME JESUS DID A REALLY DIRTY JOB FOR HIS FRIENDS IN JOHN 13:3-5 AND 12-17. BUT WAIT! BEFORE READING, TAKE OFF YOUR SHOES AND RUN AROUND OUTSIDE BAREFOOT THROUGH THE DIRT AND MUD FOR A FEW MINUTES. THEN SIT DOWN SO YOU CAN GET A GOOD LOOK AT YOUR SUPER DIRTY FEET WHILE YOU READ!

FRiENDS
ACCEPT EACH OTHER.

FACE 2 FACE

Shailene
00:31

THE FRIENDSHIP COLLISION

Lily's summer hadn't gone exactly as planned. True, staying with Emma had turned out to be a lot of fun. But there were days when Lily couldn't help thinking she ought to be at dance camp. Her parents had signed her up for an intensive month-long workshop to prepare her for an audition with one of the city's top dance troupes by the end of the summer. But the only dancing Lily had done recently was when they all broke out in the chicken dance while running a five-year-old's birthday party.

Lily tried to explain her summer as she video-chatted with her friend, Shailene, but it was hard to find the right words. "Emma's . . . I don't know, different. She rewires toasters and programs apps on her phone and stuff."

"Oh." Shailene's tone seemed to say she didn't think much of that. Lily plowed ahead, anyway. "And she hangs out with these other kids. Ethan's into rock climbing and stuff and Marco's family is from Colombia."

"Are they, like, cool?" Shailene questioned doubtfully.

"Well . . . " Lily trailed off. She didn't think Shailene would qualify their treehouse and secret missions as "cool." A month ago, Lily wouldn't have thought they were cool either. But Shailene jumped in before she had a chance to continue. "Don't say a thing, I totes get it. Anyway, don't worry about them, 'cuz I'm coming to visit! Your mom and your aunt set it up."

"Wow!" Lily exclaimed. Her mind immediately jumped to everything she and Emma had planned for the next week. Shailene could see firsthand what it was all like. "That's awesome," Lily added. "Me and Emma got hired to do this birthday party with a Peter Pan theme, so you can help, too . . . "

"Peter Pan?" Lily could practically hear Shailene rolling her eyes. Maybe Peter Pen was a little young. Lily backtracked quickly; she didn't want Shailene to think she'd changed or anything. "I'm, you know, just going along with it," she explained.

"Whatevs," Shailene responded. "I so can't wait to show you my new e-Touch 8. Dad got a pre-release model!"

Lily knew she should be excited. But for the next few days, she couldn't help wondering what Shailene would think of everything her friends said and did. Her worst fears were realized when Shailene stepped out of Aunt Liz's car and wrinkled her nose as if something about the whole neighborhood smelled bad.

When Lily ushered Shailene toward Ethan's garage to meet the gang, Shailene stared in surprise. "You hang out in a garage?"

"Ethan's mom lets us use it for our party-planning business," Lily explained. "We're trying to earn money for gear to find out what's um . . . behind this really tall fence. . . . "

Shailene simply stared. Lily had gotten just as excited as her new friends about discovering what was being built behind the fence in the woods. But now Shailene was shaking her head in disbelief.

"You've gone all 'Blue's Clues.' And what's that thing you're wearing?" Shailene pointed to the guitar picks strung on a chain around Lily's neck.

"Nothing," Lily said as she tugged off the necklace from her grandfather and balled her hand around it. Quickly, she opened the door.

"Hey, y'all!" she called brightly to her friends, and then paused. Did saying "y'all" make her sound goofy to Shailene? "I mean . . . guys," she added and ushered her friend from New York into Ethan's garage. "This is Shailene."

Lily's friends all smiled and said "hello," but it was clear they were on a mission to prepare for their Peter Pan birthday party gig.

Ethan held up a harness of ropes and rock climbing gear. "Lily, we thought you could actually be Peter Pan for the party!" he announced.

"Since you dance and everything," Emma added. "Ethan's got it all figured out, how you can be up in a tree in the backyard—"

"And we will make you fly!" Marco cut in, soaring his hands through the air to demonstrate.

Lily sneaked a peek at Shailene. Sure enough, she was rolling her eyes. Lily swallowed. "I'm, uh, not so sure about this whole Peter Pan thing. . . . "

Emma's eyes widened. "But it was your idea!"

This time, Shailene raised her eyebrows as she stared at Lily and asked, "Play pretend? Seriously?"

Lily's hands were sweating. She set down her chain necklace by a stack of party hats and rubbed her palms against her jeans. This was a disaster. The next four days were going to be a nightmare. "I think I should show Shailene . . . something else," she mumbled.

"But we need you to help if we're going to be ready in time!" Emma protested.

Shailene shook her head impatiently. "Oh, come on, Lily. We'll get your aunt to take us to the mall."

"Um, yeah. Sure!" Lily agreed, grateful for an excuse to leave. She quickly ushered Shailene out, avoiding the disappointed glances of her friends. They just didn't get it.

But when Lily found Aunt Liz, she was painting the back deck and couldn't take them to the mall. Lily and Shailene ended up on the front porch swing. "This place is a drag," Shailene muttered as she fiddled with her shiny new e-Touch 8, trying to make it work.

Lily scraped her toes along the boards of the porch, wishing she could make Shailene understand. She knew how everything must look to Shailene, because that's how it had looked to her at first,

too. Finally, she tried to explain, "It's actually been . . . kind of okay."
Shailene smirked. "Little kid dress up?! You've got to be careful
who you hang out with, Lily. We're starting middle school! You
don't want to, like, get all lame over the summer."

Lily tried to stand her ground. "Well, I'm staying here, so I kind of
have to hang out with Emma."

A stick cracked, and Lily glanced up to see Emma standing right
by the front porch. Her eyes showed hurt, but she held out Lily's
necklace in her hand.

"You forgot this," Emma said.

Lily could see Ethan and Marco watching from next door. She
rubbed her hands on her jeans again. "Oh, um. Thanks."

Flushing, Lily took the necklace back. The top guitar pick gleamed
in the sunlight as she silently took in the words engraved on it.

"Agree with each other. Don't be proud. Be willing to be a friend
of people who aren't considered important. Don't think that you
are better than others."

"It looks like you're accessorizing from the dollar store!" Shailene
scoffed.

Emma quickly jumped to Lily's defense. "That's from Lily's
grandpa!"

Lily nodded. "Grandpa George wanted to remind me how to be
a good friend here."

Shailene tossed her hair. "If you want to keep your friends at
home," she snapped, "you better think twice about the kind of
friends you make here."

Lily winced. Maybe her new friends here didn't dress super cool or know all the newest dance moves. But they did have amazing imaginations. And they had welcomed Lily as one of them.

Everyone was still watching Lily. She took a deep breath and smiled at Shailene. "I have thought twice. Emma and Ethan and Marco *are* my friends. They accepted me, even when I was new here. And kinda different."

Emma smiled and gave Lily a thumbs up. Shailene crossed her arms; she seemed to have a hard time finding a response. "Yeah . . . okay?"

"Great!" Lily announced. "Because I'm going to go finish planning a Peter Pan birthday party with my friends. And since you're one of my friends, you're welcome to help, too."

Shailene hesitated, but Emma grinned as she stared at the gadget in Shailene's hand. "Is that the new e-Touch 8?"

"Yeah, but the settings are all messed up," Shailene mumbled. "I can't make it work."

"Come help out with the party," Emma suggested. "I'll get your e-Touch sorted out when we take a break!"

Lily grinned. "Yeah, and Shailene can be Tinkerbell. She's an even better dancer than I am."

Shailene rolled her eyes, but she stood up to follow them. Emma and Lily exchanged smiles. They couldn't be sure yet whether Shailene would warm up. But they knew that whatever happened, their own friendship would stay strong. ■

DAY 2

Let's say there's a new kid in your class. Use the space below to draw a picture of a new kid you would want to be friends with and another picture of a new kid you would definitely not want to be friends with.

There are certain things that make it easy for you to be friends with someone. Like, if that person has the game you've been eyeing at the store or is really into reading the same book series you are. And there are some things that make it not so easy to be friends with someone. Like, if that person smells very bad or is mean to people.

And that's okay. We don't have to be best friends with everyone we meet. But we *do* have to be friendly to and **accept** everyone we meet. In the Bible, Romans 12:16 tells us:

> *Agree with each other. Don't be proud. Be willing to be a friend of people who aren't considered important. Don't think that you are better than others.*

Wow, that's a lot of stuff to do! Agree with each other—don't fight. Be willing to be everyone's friend—just because you think you can't be friends with someone at first doesn't mean that person won't make a great friend in the end! And don't think you're better than someone—don't look down on another person, no matter how smelly they are!

It all comes down to acceptance. **Friends accept each other.** And even if you aren't friends with someone, it's important to accept everyone. Even though you may not be friends, you can still be friendly. You can still show God's love to each person you meet.

❷ TAKE A FEW MINUTES TO THINK ABOUT FIVE THINGS YOU CAN DO TO BE FRIENDLY TO EVERYONE AND SHOW YOU ACCEPT THEM—EVEN IF YOU AREN'T THEIR FRIEND. IT CAN BE AS SIMPLE AS A GENUINE SMILE OR HOLDING THE DOOR. WRITE YOUR IDEAS HERE:

1.
....

2.
....

3.
....

4.
....

5.
....

DAY 3

No matter how hard you try, sometimes you get it wrong.

You drop the bag of groceries in a mud puddle.
You try to lather up the dog with hand lotion instead of shampoo.
You wreck your best friend's bike.

Messing up is a terrible feeling. But there's one thing that can flip the whole situation: *when someone sees your mistake and gives you a second chance anyway.*

THINK ABOUT A TIME WHEN YOU MESSED UP AND SOMEONE GAVE YOU A SECOND CHANCE. WRITE DOWN WHAT HAPPENED AND HOW IT FELT TO GET A SECOND CHANCE.

....

....

....

A man named Saul in the New Testament was given one of the most incredible second chances ever.

See, Saul had heard all about people who followed Jesus, and he didn't like them. In fact, he made it his mission to find Christians and put them in jail!

Pretty big mess up, huh?

One day, Saul was traveling to Damascus to arrest more Christians when God spoke to him in a dramatic, knock-you-to-your-knees kind of way. Saul was blinded—but for the first time in his life, he truly saw the terrible things he had done.

Now Saul was in the dark . . . and in desperate need of someone to accept him and give him a second chance.

Find a Bible or a Bible reader app, and then go to the darkest place in your house, like a closet or a bathroom with no windows. (If you're using a regular Bible, take a flashlight, too.)

Are you there? Great. After you finish reading this, turn off the light. Sit in the dark for a minute or two and imagine what it would have been like to be Saul, completely blind and staying in a city where many people knew he had planned to arrest them.

Then, turn on your flashlight or your Bible reader app and read Acts 9:1-19. See what happened when someone gave Saul—who later went by the Greek version of his name, Paul—a second chance. It may just encourage you to **go above and beyond when you accept others.**

❂ READY . . . SET . . . LIGHTS OUT!

DAY 4

Take a look at the list below. Circle the words that describe people you'd want to hang out with.

Honest	**Trustworthy**	**Sneaky**	**Popular**
Nerdy	**Liar**	**Funny**	**Strong**
Generous	**Athletic**	**Self-centered**	**Kind**
Creative	**Smart**	**Happy**	**Mean**
Cheater	**Wise**	**Loyal**	**Gossiper**

Those were probably pretty easy. When it comes to people you want to be around, there are qualities that are no-brainers.

Everyone wants to hang out with fun, happy people who are pretty smart and aren't always talking about themselves.

But what about the people who aren't nice, who talk behind people's backs, who make unwise choices, or who just aren't like you? How should you treat them?

Sometimes in order to know how you should treat others, it's best to look at how Jesus treats you. Take a look at Romans 15:7:

> **Christ has accepted you. So accept one another in order to bring praise to God.**

Jesus has accepted you. **You.** The one with the smelly feet. The one who hides the veggies under a napkin to sneak them into the trash. The one who doesn't always get along with siblings or friends or teachers or parents.

Jesus has accepted *all* of you.

It may not seem like a lot. But think about it. Jesus is God. He created everything you see. He gave you life. He loved you so much that He came to earth and died to pay for your sins.

Jesus. Accepts. You.

It's awesome. And it's how you should treat others. **Accept others because Jesus accepted you.**

So, here's the challenge. Be honest and think of a few people who are hard for you to accept. Write down those names here:

....

Why is it hard to accept them?

....

....

Now, write down a few ways you can accept them. It could be something as simple as smiling at them on the playground or saying, "Hi" when you pass them in the hallways. You might even get courageous and invite them to church. You don't have to write something big, but at least write down a few ideas to get you started.

....

....

....

This doesn't mean that you need to become everyone's BFF. You're not always going to be friends with everyone, but you can find a way to show everyone that you accept them and want the best for them.

❯ WHEN YOU ACCEPT OTHERS BECAUSE JESUS ACCEPTED YOU, YOU NEVER KNOW, IT COULD TOTALLY CHANGE THEM. AND YOU MAY JUST FIND A BFF AFTER ALL.

DAY 5

Stop what you're doing. Head to your bedroom or game room. Oh, and bring this book with you, of course.

Are you there? Good. Find a bunch of video games or board games or toys or dolls. Get them all out and lay them out on the floor. Now, put them in order from your most favorite to your least favorite.

Why did you put them in that order? Are some games just more fun to play? Do you like Mario better than Sonic or *Apples to Apples* better than *Mouse Trap*? Whatever the reason, you have certain things you like more than other things. And because of that, you play those games a lot. Maybe you even take better care of them and always make sure they're cleaned up and back on a shelf so they don't get scratched or broken.

It makes sense. They're your favorites.

But how about people? You probably have a list of people who you like hanging out with. You might even call them your best friends. Do you treat them differently than other people you know? Or the "popular" kids, what about them? Even if they aren't your friends, do you show them a little more attention than you show kids who aren't as cool?

Check out this verse from James 2:

> **My brothers and sisters, you are believers in our glorious Lord Jesus Christ. So treat everyone the same. (James 2:1)**

After this verse, James gives an example: Suppose someone is having a meeting and two people walk in. The first person has a lot of money and shows up wearing the best of the best. The other person is poor and wearing hand-me-downs with rips in the knees. The person in charge gives the best seat in the house to the rich guy, but he makes the poor person sit on the floor.

Not cool.

On the other hand, God created everyone. Jesus died for everyone. **He treated everyone the same.** James is saying you should do that, too.

You're going to have friends who are best friends, but that doesn't mean you ignore everyone else or treat them like garbage because they're not like you.

◉ INSTEAD OF RANKING YOUR FRIENDS LIKE YOU RANK YOUR FAVORITE GAMES, TREAT EVERYONE THE SAME. AFTER ALL, IT'S HOW YOU'D WANT TO BE TREATED, TOO.

AN EVENING EXPEDITION

Ethan and Marco ripped open the large delivery box as Lily and Emma watched. Ethan held up a set of grappling hooks.

"Now I can climb The Fence!" he announced.

"And attach a ladder for the rest of us," Marco added.

After weeks of planning and earning money for gear, the four friends were finally ready to tackle the 12-foot tall fence on the other side of the woods and discover what was being built beyond it.

Lily toyed with her chain strung with guitar picks. "Can't we just go around it?" she asked.

"Ethan and I tried," Emma explained. "But there's this deep ravine with a river one way."

"And a huge mess of blackberry brambles in the other direction!" Ethan pointed out.

"I guess we do have to go over," Lily admitted. "Shailene would think we're crazy," she added with a giggle. Lily's friend from New York, Shailene, had stayed for nearly a week before returning home. Though she had warmed up to the group a little, she had definitely not gotten as far as climbing trees and getting dirty.

"What do you think we will find, amigos?" Marco wondered.

Ethan struck a superhero pose. "Whatever it is, I can take it on!"

Just then, a text popped up on Emma's phone. "Uh oh," she noted. "Mom's got supper ready. We'll just have to go after."

Ethan quickly dropped the pose and glanced nervously at the sky. The sun was already dropping toward the horizon. He tried to keep his voice steady as he asked, "But . . . what if it gets . . . you know . . . late?"

Marco watched him curiously. "We will have hours still before it gets dark. If that is what worries you."

Ethan started to protest, but Emma waved them along. "Oh, come on. We're wasting time!" she announced.

As soon as the four friends had finished supper, they set out for the treehouse—their mission headquarters. Once there, Ethan arranged his gear, and Emma doled out walkie-talkies with headsets. They could hear the distant noise of heavy equipment and ringing hammers.

"Listen, that's it!" Emma pointed north. "That's the construction site."

The sun was already sinking down toward the trees. Ethan cleared his throat and said, "We better get going before it gets dar—, I mean, before we're tired."

He started down the path, but Marco jumped into the lead. "If we go off the trail we will get there much faster!"

Marco stepped off the path, heading in the direction of the distant construction sounds.

"We didn't go that way before," Emma cautioned, but Lily was already plunging into the woods after Marco. "Oh, where's your sense of adventure?" she teased.

Emma followed, holding up her smartphone. "We can always use my GPS!" she agreed.

Reluctantly, Ethan followed. But though the friends could still hear the construction sounds as they scuffed through dead leaves and hopped over fallen branches, they didn't seem to be getting any closer.

"I'm thirsty," Emma complained.

Lily's long, silky hair snagged in the brush. She jerked it loose. "Ow!" she exclaimed. "That hurt."

Ethan didn't say anything, but he watched the lengthening shadows with an anxious eye. The sun was starting to set.

"We are getting closer," Marco encouraged them. "I know it."

Without warning, the distant construction noises stopped. The workday must be over. Ethan could feel his heart pounding. "Great," he snapped. "Now, we don't have a clue where we're going!"

Lily spotted something shiny in the brush: her hair clip. "Look at this!" she pointed out. "I think we've been going in circles, anyway. What about the GPS, Emma?"

Emma frowned at an app on her phone. "I can't see the trail because of all the trees . . . " she muttered.

Marco crossed his arms and lifted his chin. "It is okay," he told them. "We will just go back the way we came."

Ethan glowered. "Yeah? Well, which way is that?" he demanded.

All four of them pointed at the same time . . . in four different directions. Fuming, Ethan stalked off by himself. This was all Marco's fault for leading them off the trail. And then the girls had to go and follow. They were just going to have to finish their adventures without him.

The others hurried to catch up with Ethan as the light dimmed. Someone snapped a branch, and Ethan jumped.

Marco narrowed his eyes. "You are afraid of the dark, amigo!" he announced.

"Well, it's your fault we're stuck out here!" accused Ethan.

"You are being, like, a big baby!" Marco shot back.

"And you're being dumb!" Ethan claimed.

"Guys, guys!" Emma shouted. They backed off, glaring at each other, as Emma held out her phone. "Look. I found the trail. It's just over there."

Sure enough, they could see the thin line of the trail a few dozen yards to their right on Emma's glowing screen.

"I will lead the way," Marco decided.

"No way," Ethan protested. "You got us lost!"

Both boys surged ahead as the girls followed. When they reached the trail, they all stalked back toward home in silence. Ethan shot a quick look at Marco, only to catch Marco glancing at him. They both glared and turned their eyes back to the path. Ethan could feel the anger boiling in his stomach. Now everyone knew he was afraid of the dark. He felt like a fool.

Lily and Emma exchanged glances.

"This is so not fun," Lily said.

"Yeah," Emma agreed. "If you guys can't get over it, me and Lily are going to start our own secret mission."

"Marco started it." Ethan grumbled.

"I did not!" Marco exclaimed.

"Okay, just stop!" Lily yelled.

Marco crossed his arms, and Ethan kicked a fallen branch. But they stopped walking. Lily tugged off her chain necklace and held it out. "Emma, can you light this with your phone?"

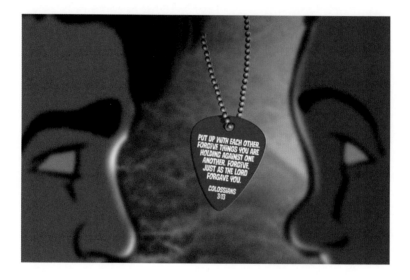

Lily flipped through the guitar picks on the necklace and held one out to Marco and Ethan. "Read it. Both of you."

After a few moments of silence, Marco took a deep breath. "'Put up with each other. Forgive things you are holding against one another—'"

"'Forgive, just as the Lord forgave you,'" Ethan finished.

Ethan wanted to stay angry. But what would it cost him? He could lose a friend. Or three! Reluctantly, he smiled. "Okay, okay. We get it," he said.

Marco's face lightened up, too. "I should not have run ahead and called you a baby," he confessed.

"Yeah. And I shouldn't have yelled at you either," Ethan admitted.

"Shake on it!" Emma told her friends.

The boys shook hands, and Emma and Lily sighed in relief.

Ethan glanced around at the near dark woods. "You know what? I really don't like the dark. Let's run!"

Laughing, the four friends sprinted for home, thankful that forgiveness could hold them together—even when things got tough. ■

DAY 2

Has anyone ever hurt your feelings or wronged you in any way? Duh. Of course they have! That's part of life. We all mess up. We all hurt others and get hurt ourselves. Sometimes by accident. Sometimes very much on purpose.

It's never fun when someone hurts you, but it's even worse when that person is a friend or someone you trusted.

Use the space below to write about the most recent time a friend has hurt you.

....

....

....

When a friend betrays your trust and hurts you in an unexpected way, it's easy to get revenge or stay mad for a long, long time. It's easy to hang it over your friend's head and remind your friend constantly of how hurt you were. But in Colossians 3:13, the Bible tells us to:

> *Put up with each other. Forgive the things you are holding against one another. Forgive, just as the Lord forgave you.*

Whoa.

Did you catch that last part? *Forgive, just as the Lord forgave you.* Now, *everyone* (even you) has hurt God in some way. You have lied, cheated, or acted in a way God didn't like. But you know what? God has already forgiven you! That's what Jesus dying on the cross was all about—forgiving you *ahead of time* for all the bad stuff you are going to do and all of the ways you are going to hurt Him.

And that verse in Colossians says we should forgive others just like God forgave us when He sent Jesus to pay the price for all our sins. So, remember that story you just wrote down? God wants you to forgive that person because **friends forgive each other.**

That person might have done something small enough that you can still be friends with them. Or maybe this person keeps doing something to hurt you, and it's best to find another friend. Forgiving someone just means that you don't hold anything against them anymore. You don't carry around a grudge or anger toward that person. Forgiveness means *letting* go of any pain or annoyance you have with someone.

❂ HOW ABOUT YOU DECIDE TO FORGIVE THAT PERSON NOW? FIND A PIECE OF PAPER (OR A FEW PIECES OF PAPER IF THERE ARE MORE PEOPLE YOU NEED TO FORGIVE) AND WRITE THE NAME OF A PERSON YOU ARE READY TO FORGIVE ON EACH SHEET OF PAPER. NOW, FOLD THE PIECES OF PAPER LIKE A PAPER AIRPLANE, GO OUTSIDE, AND LET THEM GO! SOAR THOSE NAMES INTO THE AIR, AND AS YOU DO, COMMIT TO LETTING GO OF ANY BAD FEELINGS YOU HAVE TOWARD THAT PERSON.

DAY 3

It's not fun being angry with someone. But sometimes it can feel even worse when they're angry with you!

Think about a time when you hurt someone or let them down—and they were really mad at you. What did it feel like? Did you keep thinking about it?

WRITE DOWN THREE WORDS OR PHRASES THAT DESCRIBE HOW YOU FELT.

....

....

....

You're definitely not the first person to feel that way. Everyone messes up. That's where forgiveness comes in. When you are forgiven for something you've done wrong, don't you feel so much better? That's because forgiveness frees you to move on, and in the same way, **forgiveness frees others to move on.**

In fact, the Bible says Peter once did something terrible to his friend Jesus. Peter had followed Jesus for about three years. They'd walked hundred of miles together, and Peter had watched Jesus do amazing miracles. Peter had even said out loud, in front of everyone, that Jesus was God's Son!

But then Jesus was arrested. Peter was afraid of being arrested too, so he snuck along behind the crowd to the place where Jesus was taken for trial.

Peter hung around outside, desperate to find out what would happen to his friend.

Other people started to notice. Someone thought they'd seen Peter with Jesus, so they asked him: "Are you one of Jesus' friends?"

Peter panicked. He didn't want to be arrested, so he did something terrible. He said that he didn't know Jesus! And he said it three different times.

Shortly afterward, Jesus was crucified—and then came back to life!

While everyone else was amazed and excited, Peter knew that he'd let Jesus down. He probably had a horrible, tense feeling in his stomach that Jesus might be angry with him.

Jesus knew exactly how Peter felt, so He made it clear that He had forgiven Peter. He even prepared breakfast for Peter and gave him the confidence to move on and do incredible things for God . . . like leading the new Church.

⊘ SO, GRAB YOUR FAVORITE BREAKFAST CEREAL, FIND A BIBLE OR BIBLE READER APP, AND HAVE A SNACK AS YOU DISCOVER THE STORY FOR YOURSELF IN JOHN 21:1-19. AND REMEMBER, FORGIVENESS FREES OTHERS TO MOVE ON, WHICH IS EXACTLY WHAT PETER DID!

DAY 4

Grab a blank sheet of paper, a pencil, and an eraser.

Make a mark anywhere on the page. Not gigantic, but big enough to see it.

Great. Now erase it. Completely. Pretty easy, right?

Now, draw another mark and add a few more to keep that one company.

Got them? Good. Now erase them. Make them disappear. Is your paper spotless again? Probably not too hard to get it clean again, right?

Now, go crazy on the page. Mark it up. Scribble. Doodle. Cover the whole page.

Is it covered? Great. Now, get out your eraser and make that page like all that scribbling never happened.

How's it going? Can you get that page paper-white again? Probably, you've noticed by now there's no way you're gonna get that page back to perfect. It's pretty much useless now, huh?

In a way, this is what happens when you choose not to forgive.

People will hurt you. That is just part of life. But you have a choice about how you respond when it happens.

Check out Proverbs 17:9:

> *Those who erase a sin by forgiving it show love. But those who talk about it come between close friends.*

When someone does something to hurt you, your first thought is probably not forgiveness. It's probably more like telling all your friends what that person did to you and seeing how many of them you can get on your side. The problem is, if you choose to respond that way, it's really hard—if not impossible—to fix what's broken and have a friendship again. But even though you can't fix what's broken, forgiving someone who has hurt you is the first step toward healing from how you've been hurt. Plus, it can be the first step toward mending your friendship. Because **when you don't forgive, you can ruin a friendship.**

It's sort of like your marked page. Each time you don't forgive, it's like adding a mark to your page. The page becomes so covered with marks that erasing them completely is impossible. The same goes for you. Eventually, you'll have so much hurt built up against others that forgiving them will become almost impossible.

Thankfully, we're not a sheet of paper that can't be erased. God forgave us, and He makes it possible for us to forgive others when they hurt us. We can choose to let it go and begin the process of erasing the hurt we feel.

❷ THIS ISN'T ALWAYS EASY. TAKE A MOMENT AND MAKE A REMINDER. USE THAT MARKED UP SHEET OF PAPER THAT WAS SO DIFFICULT TO ERASE. GRAB A MARKER AND WRITE OUT PROVERBS 17:9. HANG IT UP SOMEWHERE YOU LOOK OFTEN—LIKE A MIRROR OR DOOR—TO REMIND YOU HOW IMPORTANT IT IS TO FORGIVE YOUR FRIENDS.

DAY 5

People keep records for everything. In fact, you've probably read a *Guinness World Records* before to discover some of the craziest records ever.

- The record for the tallest living man is 8'3".
- The record for the most soccer ball juggling by a girl is 339 touches.
- The record for longest ears on a dog are both over 13 inches each.
- The heaviest limousine weighs in at over 50,000 pounds.
- At 5,631 and counting, someone holds the world record for owning the most rubber duckies.
- The narrowest street is in Germany and is only one foot across.
- And of course you need to know that the largest whoopee cushion is 10 feet in diameter.

Maybe you keep track of things yourself. Maybe you know exactly which LEGO® minifigures you own or how many baskets you've made since you started playing basketball. You may even have a record of every episode of your favorite TV show you've watched.

People like to keep track of stuff. It's no wonder when Paul was writing his letter to the church at Corinth, he talked about keeping records.

1 Corinthians 13:5b:

[Love] does not keep track of other people's wrongs.

When it comes to loving your friends, you shouldn't keep track of all the things they do that frustrate you. You shouldn't even keep track of the wrong things they do, period. It's not how love works.

Take how God treats us for example. Think about all of things you do wrong every day: every bad word; that time you called your sister four-eyes; and the quiz you just happened to see the

answers to on your neighbor's test. All of that, and a lot more. You would have a pretty long list if you tried to keep track of it all, huh? What's so amazing is that because of what Jesus did on the cross, God forgives all of that. And He chooses to forget it. It's like He doesn't even see it anymore.

Not like it's gonna be easy or anything, but **forgiveness means letting go of what someone did to you.**

So, when you feel like you are starting to keep a record of what people have done wrong, try this:

Take out a blank sheet of paper.

Write down everything the person did that hurt you.

Write down what you lost because of what that person did to hurt you. Maybe you lost feeling good about yourself. Maybe you lost the desire to be their friend. Maybe you lost your Xbox game because they destroyed it. Whatever they cost you, write it down. Grab a red marker and write over top of it: "I CHOOSE TO LET IT GO!"

Crumple up the page and slam-dunk it into a trashcan.

⊘ FRIENDSHIP IS ALL ABOUT LOVING ONE ANOTHER; AND LIKE PAUL SAID IN HIS LETTER, LOVE DOESN'T KEEP TRACK OF WRONGS. BEING A GOOD FRIEND MEANS BEING ABLE TO FORGIVE. AND FORGIVENESS MEANS LETTING GO OF WHAT SOMEONE DID TO YOU.

FACING DOWN THE FENCE

Ethan and Emma stared up at the heavy board fence that rose 12 feet above them. Marco and Lily crowded in close behind. The sounds of heavy machinery and the ringing of hammers filtered through the trees.

"I can't believe we're totally gonna find out what's back there!" Lily crowed.

Ethan began strapping on his rock climbing harness. "Here goes!" he announced.

Lily handed over the grappling hooks and rope, while Emma checked Ethan's walkie-talkie. Marco pulled a rope ladder from his pack. "I will throw this, amigo," he told Ethan, "when you are at the top!"

Ethan took a deep breath. After weeks of hard work, they were finally here, ready to discover the secrets behind The Fence! Pulling back his arm, he threw a hook attached to a rope. The hook locked into place over the top of the fence! Grinning, Ethan tugged on a pair of hand guards and gripped the rope. Inch by inch, he began scaling The Fence.

"Oof. This . . . is . . . hard," he croaked as his feet strained inside his climbing shoes, connecting with the rough wood.

"You've totally got it," Lily called out.

The friends watched in tense silence as Ethan crept up the boards. Ethan's eyes focused on the planks, but he could see the top of the fence at the edge of his vision. He was just four feet away now. Three feet!

But as he took another careful step, an irritating buzz interrupted his concentration. Something was circling his head and tickling his ear.

"Uh oh," he moaned. "There's a bee . . . "

What if it stung him? Desperate to get rid of it, Ethan released the rope with one hand to swat at the bee.

But in that split second, he lost his grip, sliding hard down the rope, swinging free! He heard his friends cry out as his knee slammed against the fence. Ethan toppled the last three feet, landing hard on the pine needles below.

"Oooouch." After a long moment, Ethan rolled over and sat up. He tried to flex his knee.

Marco offered a hand. "Are you all right?" he asked.

Ethan nodded, but he winced as he rose and tried to take a step. Pain shot up his leg. "My right knee," he pointed. "It's twisted."

"We totally have to take you back home," Lily announced.

But Ethan couldn't imagine giving up now when they were so close. "No way," he protested. "Not after we've come this far!"

The other three friends exchanged glances. "None of us know how to climb with gear like that," Emma pointed out.

"C'mon," Ethan pleaded. "We can do this together. I bet Lily's chain has something to say about it!"

"Yeah, okay," Lily said, and tossed him the necklace. The guitar picks clattered together, their printed verses flashing in the sunlight.

Ethan flipped through them. "Here. Perfect. It's from 1 Thessalonians 5:11. 'So cheer each other up with the hope you have. Build each other up. In fact, that's what you are doing.'"

Emma smiled. "Okay, so I *hope* your knee gets better."

Ethan pointed out a tall, sturdy oak nearby. "Lily could climb that oak tree!"

Lily frowned. "The one with that long branch? You've to got be kidding."

Marco's eyes lit up. "It goes right out over The Fence!"

"I don't know." Lily wavered. Sure, she was used to some daring moves with dance. But not 12 feet in the air! "Look how far apart the branches are," she pointed out. "You guys sure haven't tried to climb it! You didn't even think about it before now."

"None of us can. But you're so good at gymnastics," Emma encouraged.

"I know you can do it, Lily!" Ethan added.

Lily glanced around at the earnest faces of her friends. They really thought she could do this! And she would be very careful. "Well . . . okay," she decided. "But I'm coming down if it seems too dangerous." Jumping, Lily caught a low branch. She swung, flipping herself up on top, where she could just barely reach the next branch. Her fingers brushed, and then she managed to catch hold.

"Very good, amiga!" cheered Marco.

"You've got it," Emma shouted.

Ethan began chanting: "Li-ly! Li-ly!"

They all joined in as Lily continued to scramble up the tree, branch by precarious branch. Their cheers seemed to fuel strength in her arms and legs, and at last, she inched her way along the sturdy branch toward The Fence itself.

"You made it!" Emma cried out.

"Can you see anything?" Ethan called.

Lily peered through the branches, straining to see. "There's a lot of leaves . . . I'm not sure. . . . "

Then something incredible happened. Just as Lily leaned forward, part of The Fence below her suddenly swung away. A hidden door! The friends stood speechless in shock as a young man with a ponytail emerged and surveyed the scene.

"Sounds pretty exciting out here," he said. Then he glanced up at Lily. "You could have just knocked, you know."

Ethan struggled to find his voice. "It doesn't look like a door!" he gasped.

"I'm Rick," the man told them, grinning. "Director of the new Living Museum. Who might you be?"

The friends gave their names in turn as Lily finished scrambling down the tree and landed on her feet.

"Excuse me, but what's a Living Museum?" Ethan asked. The others nodded, fascinated.

"This one is mostly outdoors," Rick explained. "We'll showcase all the wildlife and plants in this area. And we're building fun rides, too. Ones that fit in with the natural landscape, like zip lines and rock climbing and river tubing."

"Wow!" Ethan exclaimed.

"So totally cool," Lily agreed.

"We're not open to the public for a few weeks yet," Rick said. "But you seem like adventurous types. Would you like a private tour?

Emma could feel a grin nearly splitting her face in two. "Yes, please!" she exclaimed.

Rick checked his watch. "I've got to meet with the foreman right now. But if it's okay with your parents, come back and knock on this door tomorrow at noon. I'll be waiting for you."

He shook hands all around and disappeared back through the nearly invisible door. The friends stared at each other, a little dazed.

"Just think," Ethan considered. "If we hadn't kept encouraging each other all summer—"

"We would never have gotten in!" Lily finished.

"C'mon, Ethan," Emma declared. "We'll help you get home and put an Ace bandage on that knee."

"Si!" Marco agreed. "So you are ready for tomorrow!"

The friends gathered around Ethan, supporting him as they began the long hike home. They couldn't wait to return tomorrow for a new adventure inside the Living Museum. ■

DAY 2

"You are such an awesome drawer!"
"I love your smile. It really brightens up a room."
"You're one of the smartest people I know."

Words of encouragement—compliments—mean a lot.

WHAT IS THE MOST ENCOURAGING THING SOMEONE HAS EVER SAID TO YOU?

....

....

....

Words of encouragement are memorable and can make your week—whether you did something you were really proud of and someone noticed and complimented it; or someone just came right out and told you something really nice they thought about you. In 1 Thessalonians 5:11, the Bible says:

> *So cheer each other up with the hope you have. Build each other up.*

Basically, **friends encourage each other.** Remember how it felt when someone said that? It probably felt like you were on top of the world for a few minutes, hours, or days. You probably kept replaying the words in your head, letting them really sink in. It may have just taken a few seconds for the person to speak the words, but for you, the words have lasted and encouraged you much longer.

Positive words that build people up are powerful. They have the ability to bring someone out of a funk—a really sad place. They can give someone the motivation to do something *big*. They can make a really bad day turn into the best day ever.

❷ SO, TAKE A MINUTE AND THINK OF A FEW PEOPLE WHO MIGHT NEED SOME ENCOURAGEMENT TODAY. DO YOU HAVE A FRIEND WHO SEEMS REALLY DOWN? IS A PARENT STRESSED OUT? HAS YOUR CLASS AT SCHOOL BEEN GIVING YOUR TEACHER A HARD TIME LATELY? WRITE THE NAMES OF THOSE PEOPLE AND COMMIT TO ENCOURAGING THEM WITH KIND WORDS IN THE NEXT FEW DAYS.

....

....

....

....

DAY 3

You probably have a lot of friends, but maybe there's one who has been your friend for the longest time.

WRITE THAT PERSON'S NAME HERE:

....

WHAT THINGS HAVE YOU OR YOUR FRIEND DONE TO MAKE THE FRIENDSHIP LAST SO LONG? WRITE DOWN ALL YOU CAN THINK OF HERE:

....

....

The Bible tells about a famous pair of friends: David and Jonathan. They actually hadn't been friends their whole lives because Jonathan was a prince and David was just a shepherd boy.

But as soon as they met, David and Jonathan became the best of friends. They promised to always look out for each other and their families.

Their friendship didn't go smoothly, though. Several times, Jonathan's father, King Saul, even tried to kill David! Still, Jonathan did everything he could to protect his friend, and David didn't reject Jonathan because of his father's wrongdoing.

Most importantly, Jonathan made it clear that David was someone of great value, even though he hadn't grown up in a palace.

First Samuel 18:1-4 tells what Jonathan did:

> *David had finished talking with Saul. After that, Jonathan and David became close friends. Jonathan loved David*

just as he loved himself. From that time on, Saul kept David with him. He didn't let him return to his father's home. Jonathan made a covenant with David because he loved him just as he loved himself. Jonathan took off the robe he was wearing and gave it to David. He also gave him his military clothes. He even gave him his sword, his bow and his belt.

Jonathan was a prince. He was next in line to become king, and he may have known already that people wanted to make David king instead of him.

Yikes!

It would have been easy for Jonathan to become jealous and angry. He could have constantly reminded David that he was really just a lowly shepherd.

Instead, Jonathan encouraged his friend and built him up. He showed David how valuable he was. He even gave David his own kingly clothes and weapons, as if to say: "You're worth it!"

You can **show your friends how valuable they are**, too! Think about one of your own friends, whether it's the one you've had longest or another friend who could use encouragement.

WHAT COULD YOU DO OR SAY OR EVEN GIVE TO THIS FRIEND TO SHOW THEM HOW IMPORTANT THEY ARE TO YOU? WRITE IT DOWN HERE.

....

....

 ◎ NOW, GET MOVING AND DO IT!

DAY 4

What's the best compliment someone has ever given you about something you're good at?

WRITE IT DOWN HERE:

....

....

Maybe someone said you are an amazing singer. Or told you that your karate kick is the best in the class. Or maybe they said the cookies *you* baked are incredible.

TAKE A MINUTE AND WRITE DOWN HOW THAT MADE YOU FEEL.

....

....

Words have power. What people say to you can put a smile on your face, make you cry your eyes out, or cause you to LOL. The same goes for the words *you* use, especially to someone who is going through a tough time.

Check out this verse from Proverbs 12:25:

> *Worry makes a man's heart heavy. But a kind word cheers him up.*

Have you ever had one of those days that was just awful? One of those days when, no matter what you did, nothing seemed to go the way you wanted?

Those are the worst, right?

Days like that happen to your friends, too. And what you say to them on days like that can make it worse, or turn it around and make it better. You can actually **use your words to encourage your friends**.

Think of your closest friends. Now pick one or two of those friends who could really use some encouragement right now. **What could you say to them to help them feel better?** Maybe it's about something you've seen them do well lately. Or an awesome way they've helped you out.

....

....

Ɔ   FIND A WAY TO TELL THEM THAT. PICK UP THE PHONE AND CALL THEM. WRITE THEM AN EMAIL. OR GO OLD-SCHOOL AND SEND THEM A POSTCARD IN THE MAIL. YOUR WORDS OF ENCOURAGEMENT MAY BE JUST WHAT YOUR FRIENDS NEED TO GET THROUGH THEIR DAY.

DAY 5

Match these famous friends and duos:

1.	Batman	A.	Jerry
2.	Buzz	B.	Brady
3.	Shaggy	C.	Tonto
4.	Lone Ranger	D.	Anna
5.	Tom	E.	Scooby
6.	Miss Piggy	F.	Donald
7.	Mickey	G.	Woody
8.	Han Solo	H.	Robin
9.	Elsa	I.	Kermit
10.	Mac	J.	Chewbacca

Look at the list above. Those are some pretty cool people who have stayed friends for a long time. Sure, they may be characters in a movie or on a TV show, but their friendships can teach us something.

Think about it. Some friendships just last longer than others. Why do you think that is?

Check out Proverbs 17:17:

> *A friend loves at all times. He is there to help when trouble comes.*

Each of those dynamic duos up top faced at least one difficult situation together. And in the face of a frozen tundra, an evil weather machine, or the Dark Side, they never gave up. They fought for each other when it got tough.

In short, they were friends at all times—even when trouble came.

It's super fun when "all times" means parties and sleepovers. But what about when it means sick and annoying?

You and your friends will face moments that just plain stink. You might want to give up and hang out with other people who don't seem to have as many problems—but stick with it, because one day you will need a friend to stick by your side when life's not so fun.

Friends stick together, even when it gets tough.

It's an easy few words to say, but sticking together—even when it gets tough—can be hard. In fact, you might not have all the answers or know what to do, but that's okay. Just be there and be ready to help out, encourage, and listen. When the time comes, you'll know what to do.

If you need help with how to deal with a friend who's going through a tough time, ask a parent, your small group leader, or another adult you trust. There are people in your life who would love to help you become a better friend. Just ask.

In the meantime, you can pray for your friends. Grab a notebook and keep a prayer journal with your friends' names and ways you can pray for them. Keep track of how God answers those prayers. You can add your own prayer requests in there, too.

⊙ WHEN YOU STICK WITH YOUR FRIENDS AT ALL TIMES, THERE'S A REALLY GOOD CHANCE THEY'LL DO THE SAME FOR YOU!

Answer Key: 1. H; 2. G; 3. E; 4. C; 5. A; 6. I; 7. F; 8. J; 9. D; 10. B

THE OTHER SIDE

Ethan and Marco followed Lily and Emma up the rope ladder into their treehouse. They all collapsed onto the floor, taking long drinks from their water bottles. Marco twisted to look at his shoulder.

"I have . . . how do you say it?" Marco considered. "Poison ivy!"

Lily examined her arms. "Just look at all these scratches from the blackberry brambles," she pointed out.

Emma winced as she tested a sore spot on her leg. "I've got bruises from the zip line," she added.

Ethan grinned at them all. "At least my sore knee is better!"

None of them really minded their scrapes. After all, they'd had an amazing five weeks, working to get the new Living Museum and Adventure Park set up. The director, Rick, had given them a chance to help when he learned they'd spent all summer attempting to discover what was beyond The Fence.

"We've gotten to try out all the fun stuff!" Emma agreed.

"Before anyone else, like, even gets to go inside!" Lily added.

It was true. Ethan had climbed the most incredible rock formation he'd ever seen and taught his friends how to start climbing, too. Emma had helped to test all the equipment in the park's communications and control room. Marco had helped to finish the dock along the river for the tubing run, and even showed Ethan how to avoid hammering his own thumb! And Lily had designed and painted the signs that pointed out each area of the park.

Now, back in the treehouse, Emma shielded her phone from the late afternoon sun as she stared at her calendar app. "How can the summer be almost over?" she moaned. "It just started!"

Lily sighed. "I have to go back to New York." Though she was eager to see her parents, and things sounded better between them, she was sad to think about leaving her new friends.

Emma nodded. "Mom and Dad are putting me in that STEM school," she noted. "So I can study tech stuff."

Ethan turned to Marco and said, "At least you and I will be starting at Logan Middle together!"

"Lo siento, amigo." Marco shook his head. "I am younger than you. Grade five."

"Fifth grade?" Emma exclaimed. "We all thought you were starting sixth grade like us!"

Lily tossed her silky hair. "We'll totally never see each other," she moaned. "What am I gonna do in the city without you guys to encourage me?" She was excited to get back to dance classes, but everyone there was super competitive. No one cheered her on like Emma and Ethan and Marco did.

"What are all of us gonna do when we can't hang out every day?" Ethan asked.

Marco frowned. "We need . . . an idea!" He popped his hand over his head like a lamp lighting up.

"Something to help us think," Emma added.

They all considered for a moment, and then, as one, turned to Lily. They all spoke at once.

"Your necklace."
"Tu collar!"
"The chain."

Lily smiled as she slid the chain, with its guitar picks and Bible verses, over her head. It was starting to be like an inside joke between them, since it always seemed to have the perfect thing they needed to hear.

"Have we read them all yet?" Ethan wondered.

Lily held out the chain so her friends could look at the verses. Emma flipped through them. "Oh, I haven't seen this one! It's from Hebrews." She read it aloud: "'Let us consider how we can stir up one another to love. Let us help one another to do good works.'"

Marco grinned. "That is what we have been doing, amigos!"

"Hey, that one's got more on the back," Lily noted.

Emma flipped it over and continued, "'Let us not give up meeting together. Some are in the habit of doing this. Instead, let us cheer each other up with words of hope. Let us do it all the more as you see the day coming when Christ will return.'"

Ethan released a long breath. "Don't really see how we can do that when we're in two different states and four different schools!"

"Wait," Emma said. "I've got it!" She clicked on her walkie-talkie and adjusted her headset. "Director Rick, this Emma. Director Rick. Come in!"

Half an hour later, the four friends had scrambled back down the ladder, up the trail, and through the hidden door in the fence. Now they stood in the Park Control Room with Director Rick.

"Looks like you've had a brainstorm, Emma," he commented.

Emma took a deep breath and laid out her plan. "Director Rick, if me and Ethan and Marco volunteer at the park for two hours each week, would you let us use the Control Room for an hour every Saturday?"

Director Rick nodded. "I'd consider it," he said. "If you have a good reason?"

Emma seated herself at the main control desk and gestured to the mics and large screens that filled the room. "If we all meet here on Saturdays, we can video chat on the big screen with Lily while she's in New York! It'll be like she's right here in the room."

Lily lit up. "I could even introduce you to my Grandpa George," she told them.

"I can tell you about the awesome new climbs I find," Ethan added.

"And what I'm learning at my new school," Emma pointed out.

"And all of the things from God that He is showing us!" Marco announced.

Director Rick smiled broadly. "I'm hearing at least five good reasons."

"So, you'll let us do it?!" Emma asked.

"Yes," agreed Director Rick. "You share your gifts here at the park, the things God has made you good at doing. And then you can use the Control Room to hang out together."

"Bueno!" Marco declared.

"Totally perfect!" said Lily.

The four friends grinned and hugged each other. They would have to go their separate ways soon enough. But that didn't mean they had to stop encouraging each other, or sharing what God was doing in their lives. ■

DAY 2

Do you have friends you can talk with about God? Maybe there are a couple of people at school, someone in your neighborhood, or maybe it's your small group at church.

WRITE THE NAMES OF THOSE FRIENDS HERE:

....

....

....

Following God can be hard. It can be a lot harder when you are the only one doing it! It's so important to have a few friends who get your relationship with God—who you can talk with about what you learned at church or what God is doing in your life.

Hebrews 10:24-25a says:

> *Let us consider how we can stir up one another to love. Let us help one another to do good works. Let us not give up meeting together. Some are in the habit of doing this.*

Just like Hebrews says, it's important to meet with people who have the same kind of relationship with God as you. It's important to talk, teach, and encourage each other when it comes to following God's Word. It's important to worship together.

Not "worship" like singing songs to God at the top of your lungs—although that can be a part of it. Worship is what you do with your life to show God and others that you love Him. When you are kind to someone, that's worship. When you serve others, that's worship. When you learn and talk about God with others, that's worship. When you live a life that makes God smile, that's worship! And **friends worship together.**

While it's important to have lots of different friends and to be friendly to everyone whether you are good friends or not, it's even more important to make time for the friends you worship with—the friends you serve and talk about God with.

For a lot of people, that's their small group at church, but maybe you have found even better friends to worship with at school or on a sports league. Whoever those people are, there are lots of ways and places you can get together regularly! And the more time you spend with these friends, the more you are worshiping God!

❂ **IN THE BOXES BELOW, GLUE PICTURES FROM A MAGAZINE OR THE INTERNET, OR DRAW FOUR PLACES YOU CAN MEET WITH THESE FRIENDS.**

DAY 3

Imagine the police knock on your door.

Imagine they drag you downtown and throw you in prison, even though you haven't done anything wrong.

Imagine that you're locked behind bars and have no idea when you'll ever be free again.

That's exactly what happened to two men named Paul and Silas! Pick up a Bible or Bible reader app and find their story in Acts 16:16-40.

> **Before reading, locate your own "prison cell." It might be a closet, the storage shed in your backyard or even the dog's crate! Crawl into "jail," and discover what happened to Paul and Silas while they were behind bars.**

Pretty crazy, right?

Paul and Silas were unfairly accused; tossed into a dark, cramped place; and locked up.

They could have whined and complained.
Screamed until their throats were raw.
Even pouted in bitter, angry silence.

Instead, they focused on what they did have: each other . . . and God. They had a party right there in the damp prison cell—singing their hearts out to God.

Paul and Silas are living proof that you can **worship together, even when you're going through difficult times.**

Worship gave Paul and Silas the courage to stay strong. It made them ready to act calmly when the earthquake freed them. It made them ready to share God's story.

Singing is just one of many ways to worship God. And it's an awesome one. God doesn't even care if you sing off key. After all, He made your voice!

❷ RIGHT NOW, GO CHECK OUT YOUR PLAYLIST OR FAVORITE CDS. CHOOSE A WORSHIP SONG AND SING YOUR HEART OUT. THEN SHARE THIS SONG WITH A FRIEND WHO'S GOING THROUGH A TOUGH TIME.

CUE UP THE MUSIC . . . AND BELT IT OUT!

DAY 4

Every language has a way to say thanks.

MATCH EACH "THANK YOU" WITH THE LANGUAGE:

1.	Thanks	A.	Hawaiian
2.	Merci	B.	Icelandic
3.	Danke	C.	Tahitian
4.	Mahalo	D.	Swahili
5.	Takk	E.	French
6.	Grazie	F.	English
7.	Mauruuru	G.	German
8.	Asante	H.	Italian

You've probably been told since you were super small to say "Thank you" anytime someone gave you something, said something nice, or invited you over to their house. Maybe you've even had to send a thank-you note to each of your friends for the birthday gifts they gave you at your last party.

Saying "Thank you" is something people all over the world do every day. And chances are, you've said it at least once today already.

Thank you—two simple words that can mean a whole lot to a friend, but might mean even more when you say them to God.

Take a look at what this songwriter told us in Psalm 95:1-2:

> *Come, let us sing with joy to the Lord.*
> *Let us give a loud shout to the Rock who saves us.*
> *Let us come to him and give him thanks.*
> *Let us praise him with music and song.*

God is great. He created the world and everything you see—and even what you can't see. Yet, He cares for even the smallest flower and bird. He knows you and loves you. He deserves worship.

Worship is like writing a thank-you note to God. It's important to **take time to say thanks to God.**

Why not take some time and do that right now?

START BY JOTTING DOWN A FEW WORDS TO DESCRIBE GOD.

....

NEXT, WRITE DOWN A FEW WAYS GOD HAS PROVIDED FOR YOU.

....

....

....

FINALLY, WRITE OUT YOUR OWN SONG OR POEM—OR EVEN A HAIKU—THAT CAN BE YOUR OWN PSALM OF GIVING THANKS TO GOD.

....

....

....

You don't have to write a song in order to say "Thank You" to God. You can sing when you're at church or in your room or in the car. You can write out your prayers of thanks in a prayer journal. Or you can simply say, "Thanks, God," when something amazing happens.

> **GOD DOESN'T TELL US HOW WE NEED TO THANK HIM. HE JUST WANTS TO HEAR US SAY "THANKS." SO TELL HIM AS OFTEN AS YOU WANT. TAKE TIME TO SAY THANKS TO GOD.**

Answer Key: 1. F; 2. E; 3. G; 4. A; 5. B; 6. H; 7. C; 8. D

DAY 5

Grab a pencil and draw a picture of your church right here.

Now, draw a picture of your small group. Stick figures are cool!

Take a look at both pictures. Now read the passage below from the book of Acts, which is the part of the Bible that tells the story of how the early church grew.

> *The believers studied what the apostles taught. They shared life together. They broke bread and ate together. And they prayed. Everyone felt that God was near. The apostles did many wonders and miraculous signs. All the believers were together. They shared everything they had. They sold what they owned. They gave each other everything they needed. Every day they met together in the temple courtyard. In their homes they broke bread and ate together. Their hearts were glad and honest and true. They praised God. They were respected by all the people. Every day the Lord added to their group those who were being saved. (Acts 2:42-47)*

Glance back at the pictures you drew. Which one of them is most like the Church, in the way it's described here?

You got it—the people. Your small group.

God didn't design the Church to be a brick building with a steeple or a big warehouse or a cute little storefront.

God made *people* to be the Church.

You.
Your friends.
Your family.

Every single person who follows Jesus is part of the Church.

And did you catch that piece about how the people felt when they worshiped with each other? It says *their hearts were glad.* God never meant for us to try to follow Him alone. He created us to find great joy in getting together with our friends and sharing our lives with them. That's why **meeting together makes us glad!**

Sure, you can be the Church when you worship with your small group on Sunday morning.

But you can also be the Church on a field trip to the zoo—when you and your friends marvel at the crazy cool creatures that God has made.

You can be the Church when you and your friends put on a car wash to raise funds for kids who don't have enough to eat.

And you can be the Church when you invite a bunch of friends over to hang out and share the awesome things you've seen God do in your life.

In fact, that's your next step.

Put together an end-of-summer cookout or potluck with your friends. Plan for everyone to bring something different to eat and their favorite game or activity to play.

❂ **THEN CELEBRATE THAT GOD IS THERE WITH YOU. CELEBRATE EVERYTHING HE HAS GIVEN YOU. CELEBRATE YOUR FRIENDSHIPS.**